*"Your mother was a very beautiful woman,
but her heart was less lovely than her face,
for it had room for only one."*

"My father," I guessed at once.

"No," Melisande answered in a quiet voice. "Your mother's heart had room in it for herself alone. When I saw this, I did the only thing I could. I made room for you inside my own heart. There you have stayed from that day to this. That is why you live in my house: because you lived first within my heart."

I felt my own heart start to thump at this. Her words had brought me pain and joy. In all fairness, I had asked for both.

"It's because I'm bald, isn't it?" I asked. "That's the reason she didn't want me."

Once
upon a
Time

GOLDEN

BY CAMERON DOKEY

SIMON PULSE
New York   London   Toronto   Sydney

SIMON PULSE

An imprint of Simon & Schuster Children's Publishing Division
1230 Avenue of the Americas, New York, NY 10020
Copyright © 2006 by Cameron Dokey
All rights reserved, including the right of
reproduction in whole or in part in any form.
SIMON PULSE and colophon are registered trademarks
of Simon & Schuster, Inc.
The text of this book was set in Adobe Jenson.
Manufactured in the United States of America
This Simon Pulse edition November 2008
2 4 6 8 10 9 7 5 3
Library of Congress Control Number 2005928863
ISBN 978-1-4169-3926-9

For the staff of Magnolia's Bookstore.
This one never would have happened without you.
And for Lissa. Even when the world seems dark,
I see the way your heart shines, golden.

PROLOGUE

It began with a theft and ended with a gift. And, if I were truly as impossible as it once pleased Rue to claim, I'd demonstrate it now. Stop right there, I'd tell you. That's really all you need to know about the story of my life. Thank you very much for coming, but you might as well go home now.

Except there is this problem:

A beginning and an ending, though satisfying in their own individual ways, are simply that. A start and a conclusion, nothing more. It's what comes in between that does the work, that builds the life and tells the story. Believing you can see the second while still busy with the first can be a dangerous mistake, a fact of life sometimes difficult for the young to grasp. When you are young, you think your eyesight is perfect, even as it fails you and you fail to notice. It's easy to get distracted, caught up in dilemmas and questions that eventually turn out to be less important than you originally thought.

For instance, here is a puzzle that many minds have pondered: If a tree falls in the forest, and there is no one there to hear it, does it still make a sound?

When, really, much more challenging puzzles sound a good deal simpler:

How do you recognize the face of love?

Can love happen in an instant, or can it only grow slowly, bolstered by the course of time? Is it possible that love might be both? A thing that takes forever to reach its true conclusion, made possible by what occurs in no more than the blink of an eye?

Yes, I think I know the answers, for myself, at least. But then, I am no longer young. I am old now. My life has been a long and happy one, but even the longest, happiest life will, one day, draw down to its close. Fold itself up and be put away, like a favorite sweater into a cedar chest, a garment that has served well for many, many years, but now has just plain too many holes to be worn.

Don't bother to suggest that I will be immortal because my tale will continue to be told. That sort of sentiment just makes me impatient and annoyed. In the first place, because the tale you know is hardly the whole story. And in the second, because it is the tale itself that will live on, not I. I will come to an end, as all living creatures must. And when I do, what I know will perish with me.

Perhaps that is why I have the urge to speak of it now.

More and more these days, I find myself thinking

back to the beginning, particularly when I am sitting in the garden. This is not surprising, I suppose. For it was in a garden that my tale began. It makes no difference that I hadn't been born yet at the time. I listen to the sound the first bees make in spring, so loud it always takes me by surprise. I sit on the bench my husband made me as a wedding gift, surrounded by the daffodils I planted with my own hands, so very long ago now. Their scent hangs around me like a curtain of silk.

I close my eyes, and I am young once more.

ONE

Here are the things I think you think you know about my story, for these are the ones that have often been told.

The girl I would become was the only child of a poor man and his wife who had waited many years for any child at all to be born. During her pregnancy, my mother developed a craving for a particular herb, a kind of parsley. In the country in which my parents were then living, this herb was called "rapunzel."

As luck would have it, the house next door to my parents' home possessed a beautiful and wondrous garden. In it grew the most delicious-looking rapunzel my mother had ever seen. So wonderful, in fact, she decided that she could not live without it. Day after day, hour after hour, she begged my father to procure her some. She must have that rapunzel and no other, my mother swore, or she would simply die.

There was a catch, of course. A rather large one. The garden was the property of a powerful sorceress.

This discouraged my father from simply walking up the house next door's front steps, ringing the bell, and asking politely if the garden's owner would share some of her delicious herb, which is precisely what he should have done. The front doorbell even possessed a unique talent, or so the sorceress herself later informed me. When it rang, the person who caused it to sound heard whatever tune he or she liked best.

Not that it made any difference, for no one ever rang the bell. To approach a sorceress by the front way was apparently deemed too risky. So my father did what everyone before him had done: He went in through the back. He climbed over the wall that divided the sorceress's garden from his own and stole the rapunzel.

He even got away with it—the first time around. But, though he had picked all the herb that he could carry, it was not enough for my mother. She devoured it in great greedy handfuls, then begged for more. My father took a satchel, to carry even more rapunzel, and returned to the sorceress's garden. But this time, though the herb was still plentiful, my father's luck ran out. The sorceress caught him with his hands full of rapunzel and his legs halfway up the garden wall.

"Foolish man!" she scolded. "Come down here at once! Don't you know it's just plain stupid to climb over a sorceress's back wall and steal from her garden, particularly when she has a perfectly good front doorbell?"

At this, my father fell from the wall and to his knees.

"Forgive me," he cried. "I am not normally an

ungracious thief. In fact, I'm not normally either one."

The sorceress pursed her lips. "I suppose this means you think you have a good reason for your actions," she snorted.

"I do," my father replied. "Will it please you to hear it?"

"I sincerely doubt it," the sorceress said. "But get up and tell it to me anyhow."

My father now explained about my mother's craving. How she had claimed she must have rapunzel, this rapunzel and no other, or she would simply die. And how, out of love for her and fear for the life of the child she carried, he had done what he must to obtain the herb, even though he knew that stealing it was wrong.

After he had finished, the sorceress stood silent, looking at him for what must have seemed like a very long time.

"There is no such thing as an act without consequence," she said softly, at last. "No act stands alone. It is always connected to at least one other, even if it cannot be seen yet, even if it is still approaching, over the horizon line. If you had asked me for the rapunzel, I would have given it freely, but as it is—"

"I understand," my father said, before he quite realized that he was interrupting. "You are speaking of payment. I am a poor man, but I will do my best to discharge this debt."

The sorceress was silent for an even longer time.

"I will see this wife of yours," she finally pronounced. "Then I will know what must be done."

Here are the things I know you do *not* know about my story, for, until now, they have never been told:

The woman who gave birth to me was very beautiful. Her skin was as white and smooth as cream. Her eyes, the color of bluebells in the spring. Her lips, like damask roses.

This is nothing so special in and of itself, of course.

Many women are beautiful, including those who don't resemble my mother in the slightest. But her beauty was my mother's greatest treasure, more important to her than anything else. And the feature she prized above all others was her hair, as luxuriant and flowing as a river in spring. As golden as a polished florin.

When my father brought the sorceress into the house, my mother was sitting up in bed, giving her hair its morning-time one hundred strokes with her ivory-handled brush. Even in their most extreme poverty, she had refused to part with this item.

"My dear," my father began.

"Quiet!" my mother said at once. "I haven't finished yet, and you know how I dislike being interrupted."

My father and the sorceress stood in the doorway while my mother finished counting off her strokes.

"Ninety-six, ninety-seven, ninety-eight . . ." The

white-backed brush flashed through the golden hair. "Ninety-nine, one hundred. There now!"

She set down the brush and regarded her husband and the stranger with a frown. "Who is this person that you have brought me instead of the rapunzel that you promised?"

"This is the sorceress who lives next door," my father replied. "It's her rapunzel."

"Oh," said my mother.

"Oh, indeed," the sorceress at last spoke up. She walked into the room, stopping only when she reached my mother's bedside, and gazed upon her much as she had earlier gazed upon my father.

"Madam," she said after many moments. "I will make you the following bargain. Until your child is born, you may have as much rapunzel as you like from my garden. But on the day your child arrives, if it is a girl, and I very much think it will be, you must swear to love her just as she is, for that will mean you will love whatever she becomes. If you cannot, then I will claim her in payment for the rapunzel.

"Do we have a deal?"

"Yes," my mother immediately said, in spite of the fact that my father said "No!" at precisely the same moment.

The sorceress then turned away from my mother and walked to my father, laying a hand upon his arm.

"Good man," she said, "I know the cost seems high. But have no fear. I mean your child no harm. Instead, if she comes to me, I swear to you that I will love her and raise her as my own. It may even be that you will see her again some day. My eyes are good, but even they cannot see that far, for that is a thing that will depend on your heart rather than mine."

My father swallowed once or twice, as if his throat had suddenly gone dry.

"If," he finally said.

"Just so," the sorceress replied.

And she left my parents' house and did not return until the day that I was born.

On that day my mother labored mightily to bring me into the world. After many hours, I arrived. The midwife took me and gave me my very first bath. Exhausted from her labors, my mother closed her eyes. She opened them again when I was put into her arms. At my mother's first sight of me, a thick silence filled the room. The sound of my father's boots dashing wildly up the stairs could be heard through the open bedroom door. But before he could reach his baby daughter, his wife cried out, "She is hideous! Take her away! I can never love this child!"

My father gave a great cry of anguish.

"A bargain is a bargain," the sorceress said, for she had come up the stairs right behind my father. "Come now, little one. Let us see what all the ruckus is about."

And she strode to the bedside, plucked me from my mother's arms, and lifted me up into the light. Now the whole world, if it had cared to look, could have seen what had so horrified my unfortunate maternal parent.

I had no hair at all. Absolutely none.

There was not even the faintest suggestion of hair, the soft down of fuzz that many infants possess at birth, visible only when someone does just what the sorceress was doing, holding me up to the light of the sun. I did have cheeks like shiny red apples, and eyes as dark and bright as two jet buttons. None of this made one bit of difference to my mother. She could see only that I lacked her greatest treasure: I had no hair of gold. No hair of any kind. My head was as smooth as a hard-boiled egg. It was impossible for my mother to imagine that I might grow up to be beautiful, yet not like her. She had no room for this possibility in her heart.

This lack of space was her undoing, as a mother anyway, for it separated us on the very day that I was born. And it did more. It fixed her lack so firmly upon my head that I could never shake it off. For the rest of my days, mine would be a head upon which no hair would grow.

But the sorceress simply pulled a dark brown kerchief from her own head and wrapped it around mine. At that point, I imagine I must have looked remarkably like a tiny walnut, for my swaddling was of brown homespun. Then, for a moment or two only, the sorceress turned to my father and placed me in his arms.

"Remember your words to me," my father said,

when he could speak for the tears that closed his throat. "Remember them all."

"Good man, I will," the sorceress replied. "For they are written in my heart, as they are in yours." Then she took me back and, gazing down into my face, said: "Well, little Rapunzel, let us go out into the world and discover whether or not you are the one I have been waiting for."

That is the true beginning of this, my life's true story.

Two

And so I grew up in the home of the sorceress.

Though not, it hardly need be said, in the house next door to the one in which I had been born. When I was still an infant, too young to remember such a thing, the sorceress and I moved to a place where gently rolling hills gradually grew steeper and more rocky until they became a great mountain range that divided the land from side to side.

There, in a fold of two such hills, the sorceress and I had a small, one-room house for ourselves, and a large, one-room barn for the livestock. Our house had a roof of thatch, and the barn a roof of sloping boards. We had an orchard of fruit trees climbing up one hill, with a rushing stream at its base. And, of course, we had a beautiful and prosperous herb and vegetable garden. Above all else, the sorceress dearly loved to help things grow. I suppose it could be said that I was one of them.

I learned much in the sorceress's home. She taught me to spin and sew. To sweep the floor of our small dwelling without raising up a single cloud of dust. To gather eggs, to separate them and make the yolks into a custard, and then to beat the whites so long and hard that I could bake a cake as white as snow, and as tall as our oven door.

Together, we helped the cows give birth, carded wool from our own sheep to create cloth. It was from the sorceress that I learned to climb the apple trees in our orchard. I even bested her when it came to baking apple pies. I learned to help rehatch the roof, a task I dearly loved, and to whitewash our walls, which I did not. Best of all, I learned to read and write, great gifts, not often bestowed upon girls at that time.

I also learned never to ask a question unless I truly wished to hear the answer, for the sorceress always replied honestly. I learned not to call her "mother." She would not allow it. Instead, as the sorceress called me by my name, so I called her by hers. It was my first word, in fact, and it was this: Melisande.

But of all I learned in the sorceress's home, sorcery was not a part. This is not as odd as you might suppose. Think of your own life for a moment. Are there truly no questions you consider asking, then reconsider, deciding you'd rather not hear the answers after all? Or perhaps the questions never even occur to you in the first place. We all grow accustomed to our lives just the way they are. For me it was a combination, I think. I'd reached the fairly advanced age of eight or nine, in fact, before I even discovered that Melisande was a sorceress at all.

It happened in this way: On a market day in late

September, the sorceress hitched up our wagon and announced that we were going to the closest town. She did not like to do so, she said. Towns were filled with people, more unpredictable than spring weather. But the last of our needles had snapped in two the night before and, without replacements, we could make no winter clothes.

"Tie your kerchief tightly around your head, Rapunzel," she said. "I will do the same."

No woman or girl went with her head uncovered in those days. It simply wasn't proper. To make sure that I had tied my own kerchief to her satisfaction, Melisande reached down and gave the knot a tug. I opened my mouth to ask why our kerchiefs needed particular attention on this particular day, then closed it again, having said nothing at all. As an interesting side benefit of learning which questions to ask and which to keep to myself, I had developed the ability to answer many on my own.

It has to do with the fact that my head is different, I thought. I would learn much more about what this meant before the day was done. In the meantime, however, I was excited, for, though Melisande had sometimes spoken of such places, I had never seen a town before.

The day was fine. By the time we reached the market square, I had a crick in my neck from trying to turn it in every direction all at the same time. I had never seen so many people assembled in one place, nor imagined how many buildings it might take to house them all. Our horse's shoes made an unfamiliar sound on the cobblestone streets.

In the center of the town stood a great open square, completely filled with stalls selling goods of every imaginable kind. Through them, I could just catch a glimpse of green grass in the very center, and the tall brick sides of a well. Water was at the heart of every town, Melisande had explained as we'd ridden along. Without water, there could be no life.

She found a place to stable the horse and cart, and we set off for the stalls.

"Stay close to me, Rapunzel," Melisande said. "The town is a big place. It would be easy for you to lose yourself."

"I won't get lost," I replied. Which, as I'm sure you've already noticed for yourself, was not quite the same as giving a promise.

For a while, though, the point was moot. I was content to stay at the sorceress's side. Wonderful and exotic goods filled the market stalls, or so it seemed to me at the time. Only the fruit and vegetable stalls failed to tempt me. They didn't hold a candle to what we grew at home. Eventually, however, Melisande fell to haggling over the price of needles, and I grew bored. I took one step from her side, and then another. By the time I had taken half a dozen, I had broken the invisible tether that tied me to her and been swallowed up by the crowd.

Even then, I had no fear of getting lost. I knew right where I was going: to that patch of green at the very center. I wanted to see what the heart of a town truly looked like. I can't say quite what I was expecting, though I can say it wasn't what I found. On the lush green grass in the center of the square, a group of town children were playing a game that involved running and kicking a ball. It was just a blown-up pig's bladder, no more special than balls I had played with myself, but it was tied with a strip of cloth more blue than any sky.

At this sight, my heart gave a great leap. I was a fast runner and knew well how to kick a ball. I had dreamed many dreams in my small warm bed at night, and wished upon many a star. The wish I had breathed most often had been for playmates. So when the ball tied with that bright cloth abruptly sailed my way, I did not hesitate, but kicked it straight to the player my eyes had gone to first and lingered on the longest: a tall lad several years older than I. Right on the cusp of being a young man. If it hadn't been a market day, he probably wouldn't have been playing at such games at all.

Instantly, my action caused a great hue and cry; of joy on the part of the lad and his team, and outrage on the part of his opponents. For, until the moment I had intervened, the ball had been in their possession, and they'd looked fair to win the day.

"Oh, well done!" the lad cried. "Now let's show 'em! Come on!"

I joined the game, running for all I was worth, which turned out to be a great deal, for all that I was small. Like a minnow in a stream, I slipped in and out of places larger fish could not go. The catastrophe occurred in just this way, as I attempted to dive with the ball through the legs of the captain of the opposing team. He pulled his legs together, trapping me between them, then reached down to capture the ball.

This, he missed, for I managed to give it a great push and send it flying. His fingers found my kerchief instead. With one hard yank, he pulled it off. The fact that I had tied the knots so carefully and tightly that morning made not one bit of difference.

My head was exposed.

The boy gave a great yelp and leaped back. Instantly the game stopped. So profound a silence fell over each and every child that the adults in the closest stalls noticed, stopped their work, and came to see what had caused the lack of commotion. Before I could so much as reach for my kerchief, I found myself completely surrounded by curious, hostile eyes.

Eight years had changed some things about the top of my head. It was no longer white, but brown, from spending time in the sun. Its most significant feature, however, hadn't changed a bit: It was still completely smooth, and I completely bald.

I could feel a horrible flush spread up my neck and over my face, one that had absolutely nothing to do with the fact that I'd just been running hard. I sat as still as I possibly could, praying that the earth would miraculously open up and swallow me whole.

It didn't, as I hardly need tell you. Instead, somebody stepped forward: the lad who had first encouraged me to join the game. He didn't look so enthusiastic now. His eyes, which I suddenly noticed were the same color blue as the cloth around the ball, had gone wide. The expression on his face was flat and blank, as if he was trying to give away nothing of what he might be feeling, particularly if that thing was fear. This I instantly understood, for I knew that to show fear was to give your opponent an advantage you frequently could not afford.

"Why do you look that way?" he asked. "What did you do wrong?"

"Nothing," I answered swiftly, responding to the second question and ignoring the first entirely.

"You must have done something," he countered at once. "You must have. You don't look right."

"No one knows that better than I do," I answered tartly. "I'm bald, not stupid or blind."

"Perhaps she is a changeling," another voice suddenly spoke up, a grown-up's this time. At these words, the entire crowd sucked in a single breath, after which many voices began to cry out, all at once.

"Stay away from her!"

"Don't touch her!"

"Pick her up and throw her in the well! That'll show us what she's made of. That's the test for witches."

"*Enough!*"

At the sound of this final voice, all others fell silent. I saw the crowd ripple, the way the rows of corn in our garden do when the wind strikes them. Then the crowd parted and through it stepped Melisande.

The expression on her face was one I'd never seen before: grief and fury and regret so mixed together it was almost impossible to tell them apart. Without a word, she walked to my side and helped me to my feet. Then she stooped and retrieved my kerchief from the ground.

"It seems those knots weren't quite as tight as we supposed," she said, for my ears alone, as she worked them free and wrapped the kerchief around my head once more. Her face was set as she tied a new set of knots herself, but her fingers were as gentle as always.

"I'm sorry," I said. "I didn't mean for it to happen."

"Of course you didn't," she replied. "There's no need for you to be sorry. You're not the one who should apologize."

At this, she turned back to face the crowd.

It's hard to describe precisely what happened then. Later I realized that I had been given my first real glimpse of sorcery. As Melisande gazed upon them, many in the crowd cried out. Some fell to their knees and covered their faces with their hands, while others stood perfectly still, as if they had been turned to stone. In the end, though, they were all the same in one thing: Each and every one of them looked down.

No person there assembled could hold the sorceress's eyes with their own.

Then she glanced down at me, and it seemed to me as if my heart would rise straight up out of my chest. All my fears were laid bare, and my hopes also. A voice in the back of my mind instructed me to look away or I would have no secrets left, but I did not. What had I to conceal? This was not some stranger, who saw only my own strangeness. This was the woman who had raised me since my birth. The only one I knew and trusted. This was Melisande.

And so I held her eyes and did not look away. After a moment, she smiled. I smiled back, and at this, my heart resumed its proper place and all was right once more.

"I thought so," she said, as she turned back to the crowd. "This girl has more courage than any of you. Have no fear. We will not come amongst you again. But I think there will be many of you who will now come to seek me out."

Then she reached down for my hand, I reached up to place mine within hers, and, together, we made our way back through the crowd. It wasn't until we were almost through it that anyone made a sound at all. And even then, it was just a single word muttered under the breath.

"Sorceress."

I stumbled, my feet abruptly growing clumsy, but Melisande's footsteps never faltered at all, though she did stop walking.

"Fearmonger," she replied. "Coward, I see what is in your heart. Be careful what you sow there, for it may prove to be your only harvest, and a bitter one at that."

She did not speak again until we reached our own door. But, though I stayed as silent as she, that single word, *sorceress*, rang in my head all the way home.

THREE

In the years that followed, some things changed.

Others did not.

The hair on Melisande's head got a little longer and began to turn gray. I turned first nine, then ten, and finally, in their proper times and places, eleven, twelve, and thirteen, and all the while the top of my head stayed as bald as any egg I could find in our henhouse.

I did blister it badly with sunburn the year I was ten, having refused to wear a kerchief or hat in a fit of pique over something I cannot now recall. But aside from that, it didn't change a bit. Mine remained a head upon which no hair would grow.

My eyes, however, functioned just fine, and I began to keep them peeled for additional signs of sorcery, watching Melisande when I was sure she didn't notice (though of course she did—not because she was a sorceress but because she was a grown-up).

She kept her eye on me; I wasn't quite sure why. But I finally figured out that she undoubtedly saw me watching her, because I began to notice that *she* was watching *me*. Her face would take on a sort of considering expression from time to time, as if she were weighing the image of me her eyes presented with one she was holding in her mind. Each and every time, at the precise moment I decided she had finally made up her mind to speak of whatever was in it, she looked away and said nothing at all.

But the biggest change of all, I suppose, was that after that day in the town, we were no longer quite as alone as we had been before.

Melisande had been quite right when she predicted that the fact that people knew there was a sorceress in their general vicinity would draw them to her, even if they were not always quite convinced that it was altogether safe for them to come. Word of her presence and her power spread, and, as it did, more and more visitors began to appear at our door.

At our back door, to be precise, which always made me smile. It made no difference that a perfectly good road came right up to our front gate. Every single person who traveled to see us for the purposes of sorcery preferred to present themselves at the back door. Some knocked loudly, boldly demanding entry. Others merely scratched, as if, even as they asked for admittance, they were second-guessing themselves and wishing they were on their way back home.

How does sorcery work, where you come from?

For I have learned, since that day in the village green when I first discovered its presence in the world at all, that the workings of sorcery are not universal. They have to do with the individual who performs them. Sometimes her powers exist to fill a great need in the land in which she lives. Other times they exist to fill a need within the sorceress herself. More often than not, of course, it's likely to be both. For sorcery is no simple thing, though simpletons often think it so.

The gift of sorcery that Melisande possessed was this: to see into the hearts of others even when they themselves could not, and to show them what she saw.

That was what she had done that day on the village green, what had caused every single person present to drop his or her eyes. She had looked into their hearts and seen their fear of me, of what I looked like, and their desire to cast me out because of it. And she had done more. For she had both seen and revealed the villagers' deepest, most secret fear of all: that my presence among them might prove infectious, bringing down upon their own heads the fate they wished for me, regardless of whether the heads in question had hair on them or not.

Some were horrified to discover their hearts could hold such feelings and fears. Others knew they were there full well and were horrified at having been found out. In the end, though, it made no difference: Not one was able to meet the message of her or his heart as seen within the sorceress's gaze. Each and every person dropped their eyes.

After such an inauspicious beginning, you might think no one would want to come to see us. But this was far from true. There were many, or so it seemed, who were willing to brave the sorceress's gaze to catch a glimpse of the innermost workings of their own hearts, never mind that it might be said they should have been figuring out a way to do this for themselves.

"Why do they come?" I finally asked one day, after a particularly disastrous departure.

A young woman, one of the loveliest I had ever seen, her beautiful features streaked with tears, had come barreling out the back door just as I had been on the point of coming in with a basket of apples from the orchard. I stepped back quickly to avoid her and lost my footing, which sent me to the ground and the basket and its contents flying.

Well, I guess I'll be making applesauce instead of pies tonight, I thought.

"What did you show her, the end of her beauty?" I asked crossly as Melisande appeared in the doorway. Together we watched the young woman hurry away, the sound of her sobs drifting back over her shoulder. "I recognize that look. It's disappointed hopes. A few more years of that and no one will remember she was beautiful in the first place. What on earth do they expect you to do for them, anyhow?"

"That is a very good question, my Rapunzel," answered Melisande. She knelt beside me and began to help me retrieve the apples, the bruises already showing on their skins. "And one I wish these fools would ask themselves before they come."

Her words startled me, I must admit. She rarely

25

spoke of those who sought her help, never passed judgement on them. I stayed quiet, gathering up the apples. I'd asked more questions than usual, but I knew that, sooner or later, she would answer them all, and answer them honestly. That was the way things worked around our house.

"They come," the sorceress said at last, "because they confuse seeing a thing with understanding it, and they believe that my true power lies in the bestowing of this shortcut."

"Then they are idiots, as well as lazy," I snorted. "For the first lies within your power, it is true, but the second may or may not. And either way, it makes no difference. A shortcut may be fine if you're walking through a field, but it hardly seems in order when you're dealing with the heart."

"Well spoken on all counts," Melisande said, and at this she smiled. "I had not thought to have you follow in my footsteps, but perhaps I should reconsider. With thinking like that, you have all the makings of a first-class sorceress."

"No, thank you," I said. "I think I'm odd enough." A quick silence fell. *Oh, excellent, Rapunzel,* I thought. *That was nicely done.* "Not that I think you're odd," I added.

"Don't be ridiculous," Melisande said. "Of course I am. I'm a sorceress, aren't I?"

"I have heard that," I said. "Though I haven't felt the need to test it for myself."

I saw the considering expression come into her face then. *Aha!* I thought. *Perhaps now I will know.*

But the sorceress simply picked up the basket, got to her feet, and said: "I'll peel the apples. The peelings will make a nice treat for the pigs. Perhaps there will be enough for pies tomorrow."

And so I learned no more on that day, and the very next, Mr. Jones came into our lives.

I have told you that I learned many things from Melisande, the exception being sorcery itself. But here I must confess one failure. No matter how hard or how often Melisande tried to teach me, I could never learn to tell one plant in the garden from another, let alone what they were called.

I was not entirely hopeless, of course. I could do the large and obvious things. I could tell an apple from a raspberry; cauliflower from corn. But when it came to knowing things by the shapes of their leaves, by what they smelled like when you plucked them and rubbed them between your palms, even whether a plant was a weed or whether it was not, these things I simply could not keep straight in my mind.

On the day that Mr. Jones came into our lives, I was working among the rows of vegetables where, insteading of ridding the carrots of weeds as I should have, I rid the weeds of carrots by pulling up every single seedling, carefully and methodically, one by one. When I realized my mistake, I sat back on my heels with a sharp cry of dismay, which caused Melisande to appear at the back door. It was open, for the day was warm and fine.

"What is it?" she called. She didn't actually say,

"this time," but then she didn't need to. I could hear it in her voice like the chime of a bell.

"Carrots," I admitted, and saw her wince, for carrots were a highly useful vegetable, good in summer, autumn, and winter alike.

"All of them?" she inquired.

"All of them," I nodded.

Even at the distance from the garden to the back door, I heard her sigh. She came over to hunker down beside me, surveying the damage.

"Perhaps it is to be expected," she murmured after a while. More to herself than to me, really. I think this may have been what finally broke open a place inside me. A place I had always suspected, but been not quite certain I wished to acknowledge, for it was a place of anger and confusion.

"You mean because I'm named for a plant in the garden?" I asked tartly. "In that case, why didn't you encourage my mother to name me for something inanimate and impossible to kill, like a cutting board or a set of fireplace tongs?"

"You'd only have dropped them on your foot, or had some other accident," Melisande replied. Her voice sounded calm, but I could see the surprise flicker across her face. "And it was not your mother who named you Rapunzel," she continued. "It was I."

Just for a moment, I felt the world tilt. This is what happens when something truly takes you by surprise. Not that I hadn't been asking about my parents, because of course, I had been. The sorceress and

I had carefully avoided the topic until now, which was as much my doing as hers. For, if I asked, I knew that she would answer, and answer honestly. This fact of life had made me very careful about what I asked, and what I did not.

"Why did you name me Rapunzel?" I inquired, after what felt like a very long moment.

Melisande was silent herself, for a moment that felt even longer than mine.

"Because it seemed the proper choice at the time," she finally replied. "Your mother ate large quantities of it before you were born. I first met your father, in fact, when I caught him stealing great handfuls of rapunzel from my garden."

"So my name is a punishment then," I said.

"Don't be silly," Melisande said. "Of course not."

I stared down the row of carrots, their tiny green tops already wilting now that they were no longer in the ground.

"Why do I live with you? Are my parents dead? Didn't they want me?"

There. I had done it. Asked the three most important and difficult questions, the ones I'd hidden away within that space I hadn't even been certain was there inside me. And I'd asked them all at once. If I could survive the answers to these, I had to figure I could survive almost anything.

"You live with me because I love you," Melisande said. "And your parents are still living, as far as I know."

"You left one out," I said, when she stopped speaking. "They didn't want me, did they? That's the real reason you took me in."

"Ah, my Rapunzel," Melisande said on a sigh. She looked up for a moment, her eyes on mine. "When you are a little older, you will realize that not all questions have such simple answers."

"That doesn't mean I won't ask them anyway," I said, at which she smiled.

"No. I'm quite certain it does not. Nor am I saying you should, just so you know. You'll soon learn for yourself that even the simplest question can be complicated, and the answer to it even more so. But very well, since you have asked, I will tell you what I know. Your mother was a very beautiful woman, but her heart was less lovely than her face, for it had room for only one."

"My father," I guessed at once.

"No," Melisande answered in a quiet voice. "Your mother's heart had room in it for herself alone. When I saw this, I did the only thing I could. I made room for you inside my own heart. There you have stayed from that day to this. That is why you live in my house: because you lived first within my heart."

I felt my own heart start to thump at this. Her words had brought me pain and joy. In all fairness, I had asked for both.

"It's because I'm bald, isn't it?" I asked. "That's the reason she didn't want me."

"Yes," Melisande said. I felt a great roaring start to

fill my head. "And no," the sorceress went on, at which the roaring stopped. "When your mother looked at you, what she wished to see was a version of her own beauty. She could not see who you might become. It was this emptiness in her that caused her to turn you away. Your bare head is the true reflection of your mother's heart."

"Well, that's not fair at all," I said.

"No," Melisande answered. "It is not. But you are not the first example of the faults of the parents being visited upon the children, nor will you be the last."

"That's comforting," I said. "Thank you very much. What about my father?" I asked after a moment. "Where was he when all this was going on?"

"Your father loves you as much as anything in the world," Melisande replied. "But he could not interfere. He had done a thing that he should not have, and a bargain is a bargain."

"Where are my parents? Will I ever see them again?"

"Those are questions to which I do not know the answers. I am sorry, my Rapunzel."

Well, that's that, I thought. I'd asked, and she had answered. Now I knew, and life would go on.

"That's all right," I said at last. "Perhaps I will go to look for them myself, for my father at least, when I am old enough. In the meantime, I think I will be content to remain what I have always been."

"And what is that?" Melisande asked.

"Just what you have said I am. Your Rapunzel," I replied.

"My Rapunzel," Melisande said. And, for the first time that I could remember, I saw that she had tears in her eyes.

"What on earth is that?" I suddenly said.

"What?"

"That," I said. "That sound."

The sorceress cocked her head. The air was filled with it now. A noise that sounded like a set of pots and pans, doing their best to impersonate a set of wind chimes.

"I haven't the faintest idea," Melisande said. "Why don't you go and find out?"

"At least we know one thing," I said, as I got to my feet.

"And what is that?"

"Whoever it is, they haven't come for sorcery. They're at the front door."

The sound of Melisande's laughter followed me all the way around the side of the house.

FOUR

There was a wagon in our front yard, the likes of which I had never seen before. Behind the driver's seat was what looked for all the world like a house made of canvas. It had a pitched canvas roof and four sturdy canvas sides. One of them actually seemed to have a window cut out of it. Lashing ropes held the sides in place, but I thought I could see how they could be raised as well, causing the house to disappear entirely when the weather stayed fine.

Along each of the sides dangled the strangest assortment of items I had ever seen. On the side nearest to me was a set of pots and pans, with a set of wind chimes right beside them. *Well, that explains the sound*, I thought. Though why a wagon such as this should have arrived at our front door, I could not possibly imagine.

"If you're looking for the town, you're on the wrong road," I said, then bit down hard on the tip of my tongue. There's a reason you're not supposed to say the very first thing that comes into your head. If you don't take the time to think through your words, you end up being rude just as often as not.

But the man in the wagon simply pushed the hat

back on his head and looked me up and down. He had a round face with a pleasant expression, for all that it was deeply lined by the sun. A set of ginger whiskers just beginning to go gray sprouted from his chin. Hair the same color peeked out from under the brim of his hat. Beneath ginger eyebrows were eyes as black and lustrous as mine.

At the moment they were blinking, rapidly, the way you do when you are trying not to cry, or you step outside on a summer's day, then step right back again because the light out there was brighter than you thought.

"I am not looking for the town," the stranger finally replied, and I found that I liked the sound of his voice. It was low and warm, a good voice for story-telling, or so I suddenly thought. "But if I were, I would know where to find it," he went on. "I am good at knowing how to get where I am going. You could say it's a necessary part of my job."

"And what is that, exactly?" I inquired.

At this, the expression on his face, which had seemed highly changeable at first, settled down and became one I recognized: surprise.

"Have you never seen a tinker before?"

"Why would I be asking if I had?" I said, then flushed, for that was twice in a row I had been rude now. But the tinker did not seem to take offense. Instead he simply tilted his head to one side, as if he were a bird and I a worm he was trying to figure out the best way to tug from the ground.

"What is your name, young one?" he inquired.

"Rapunzel," I replied. "And I'm thirteen, just so you know." And it was only as I felt my name in my own mouth that I realized that I had never had to answer this question before, for no one had ever inquired of me who I was.

To my surprise, the tinker's face changed once again, this time growing as flushed as mine. His hands tightened upon the reins still resting in his lap, so that the horse that pulled the wagon whinnied and tried to back up into the wagon itself. At this, the tinker dropped the reins, got down from his place, and moved to the horse's side. He soothed her with gentle voice and hands and produced a carrot from deep within some hidden pocket.

"You are skilled in plant lore, then?" he asked at last. His face had resumed its former color, though he did not look at me again. Instead, his eyes intent upon his task, he offered the carrot to the horse on one flat palm.

I gave a snort.

"Far from it. As a matter of fact, I'm completely hopeless. I've just spent the morning yanking up every single carrot in the garden. Not on purpose, though," I added quickly.

At this, the tinker's face began a war with itself. I realized what the battle was about when he lost it and began to smile.

"Perhaps I might interest you in a packet of seeds, then," he suggested, as the horse finished up its treat and began to nuzzle at the tinker's legs for more. "To help you recover from your losses of this morning. To have no carrots is a terrible thing. What will you do for stew in the wintertime?"

"That's a very good question," I said. "And one I'm sure Melisande has been pondering."

"Melisande," the tinker echoed. "That is your mother?"

"No," I answered honestly. "But I love her as if she were, which makes her much the same thing, I suppose. If you will step around the back of the house, I will take you to her, and draw you a dipper of water from our well. You must be thirsty, and your horse as well. If you come down our road, you have come a long way, even if you weren't trying to end up in the town."

"Well said," Melisande's voice suddenly floated across the yard. "I'm pleased to see you finally remembered your manners."

At the sound of her voice, the tinker looked up and found the place where Melisande stood with his eyes. I held my breath. The tinker held the sorceress's eyes. And it seemed to me, in the moments that followed, that I caught my second glimpse of sorcery.

The very air around us seemed to change, solidifying and becoming thick and glossy. It reminded me of the pieces of glass that Melisande and I had swept up last winter, when a limb from one of the apple trees had come loose and been blown all the way across the orchard, only to come crashing down against the windowpanes of our greenhouse. The broken pieces were just the way the air was now. Thick and clear enough to see right through, but also sharp enough to cut you.

"Good day to you, sorceress," the tinker said finally.

"And to you, traveler," Melisande responded. "You have come a long way, I think."

"I have," the tinker acknowledged. "But I do not mind the miles, for I think that, in this place, they will now be well rewarded."

The air began to waver, then. Rippling like water.

"As to that, I cannot say," Melisande answered softly. "But I will say this: I hope it may be so. In the meantime, however, I can say this much more: Wherever we dwell, you will be welcome."

And, just like that, the air returned to normal. It was, in fact, so completely like itself that I found myself wondering if I had imagined the entire episode. The air does not change its substance, as a general rule. Unless you count things like rain or snow.

"Your words are both kind and honest," the tinker said. "A difficult combination to manage, I think. I thank you for them."

You didn't imagine anything, Rapunzel, I thought. For, even though my young ears were young, they could still detect that there was much more being said here than what was being spoken.

"I will see to your horse, if you like," I offered.

"Thank you," the tinker said with a nod.

But as I went to free the horse from its tracings, a commotion occurred within the wagon, a great cater-wauling of sound. A moment later, a small orange kitten burst out the front, as if fired from a gun. It took two great leaps, landing first upon the horse's back, and then upon my shoulder.

Once there, it turned swiftly, hissing and spitting, just in time to face a long-nosed terrier that thrust its head out from between the fabric at the wagon's entrance and began to bark in its best imitation of a larger, more ferocious dog.

"I don't suppose you'd care to have a cat?" the tinker inquired over the sound.

As the kitten's claws dug into my neck, I winced and met Melisande's eyes. Our old mouser, Timothy, had died over the winter, and I missed him sorely, though the mice did not.

"Rapunzel," Melisande said.

"Thank you," I said, on a great rush of delight. "We'd love one." Precisely as if the kitten had understood my words, it removed its claws from my neck, turned around twice more, then sat down upon my shoulder, as if ending up right there had been its intention all along, and began to lick one ginger paw.

"Excellent. That's settled, then," the tinker replied. He moved to silence the terrier, who was well on its way to yapping itself hoarse.

"Rapunzel," Melisande said. "Perhaps you should introduce the cat to the barn."

"What will you name him?" the tinker called after me. The terrier, feeling it had won the day, retired back inside the wagon and order was restored.

I turned and regarded the tinker's ginger whiskers for a moment. I had never been offered the opportunity to name a living thing before. It was a big responsibility, and I wanted to make the right choice.

"How are you called?" I finally asked, as an idea took shape in my mind.

"Mr. Jones."

"Then that's what I'll call him, too," I said. "So that I may always remember you for this gift. Also, your hair is the same color."

At this the tinker gave a laugh, Melisande smiled, and I knew I had done well. And that is how I acquired two new friends in the very same day, and both of them named Mr. Jones.

Late that night I came suddenly awake, my body sitting straight up in the darkness before my mind had the chance to understand why. I stayed still for a moment, listening hard with both my ears. I had not been prone to nightmares, even when I was small. So it never once occurred to me that I might have been roused by some phantom. If I had awakened, it was for a good cause.

I listened to Melisande's quiet breathing, coming from across the room. The tinker, Mr. Jones, had shared our supper and was now asleep in his own wagon, which still stood in our front yard. I heard the wind moving through the trees in the orchard, the faint clank it raised from the items on the tinker's wagon. *Not these*, I thought. For these had helped lull me to sleep in the first place. And that was when I heard it: the stamp and blow of the horses in the barn.

In a flash I had thrown back the covers and leaped out of bed, causing the kitten, Mr. Jones, to send up a protesting meow. I snatched up the clogs that always sat by the side of my bed when my feet weren't in them, and moved swiftly to the front door. There I slipped the clogs on, pulled my shawl from its peg, and tossed it over my head and shoulders. Then I opened the door as quietly as I could and eased out into the yard.

The tinker's wagon was a great lumpen shape in the moonlight. I could hear the horses more clearly now. I had put the tinker's horse in with our own, so that they might be company for one another. I might be a total loss when it came to the garden, but I was good with animals of all kinds. And so I knew the cause of the sounds as clearly as if the horses had spoken and told me what was happening themselves.

There was an intruder in the barn.

You will wonder, I suppose, why I didn't take the time to summon Melisande or Mr. Jones. But the simple truth is that, in the heat of the moment, it never even occurred to me. I was the one who had heard the horses. It was up to me to settle the situation on my own. If I had been older, I might have recognized my own danger and taken an indirect approach. But I was young, and the shortest distance between two points was still a straight line. And so I marched straight over to the barn and slid its great door open as far as I could. For if there is one thing upon which a thief relies, it is stealth.

"You'd better get away from those horses," I said in a loud, strong voice. "Or I'll make you. I can do that, you know. I'm a powerful sorceress."

"You are not."

I'm not sure which one of us jumped the higher, me or the boy. For that's who it was inside the barn. A lad, a year or so older than I was by the look I got of him in the moonlight. Chin lifted in defiance, though I noticed he was not quite as close to the horses as I thought he'd been when I first opened the barn door. Even the threat of sorcery will do that to a person.

"Am too," I said. "I'll prove it if you don't watch out."

"You're not the sorceress," he insisted. "The other one is. Be quiet, will you? Just come in and close the door. I'm not stealing anything, I promise."

"Only because I caught you before you could," I said right back. But I did step in and slid the door partly closed behind me. To this day, I can't quite say why. There was something in his expression that I recognized, I think. Some sort of longing, mixed in with all that defiance.

"Well?" I said. "I'm waiting for an explanation."

He put his hands on hips at this. "And you can

keep on waiting. Just who do you think you are?"

"I could ask you the same question," I remarked. "In fact, I think I have the right. You're the one standing in my barn."

"I'm Harry," he said, after a moment's consideration. "And I'm running away."

"In that case, I'm Rapunzel," I said. "And not with our horse, you're not."

"I'll take the tinker's horse, then," the lad named Harry offered. "He'll never miss it. He has lots of other things."

"He most certainly will miss her," I said, for the horse was a mare, and in the course of the afternoon I had grown fond of her. "Particularly when he has to pull the cart himself." I took a step closer, studying Harry's features. "Why should you wish to steal from the tinker? He seems nice enough."

"He took me away from my parents," he said, after a slight hesitation.

"*What?*"

"It's true. He did," Harry blustered.

"No," I said. "That can't be right. Or even if it is, there must be more. If he was as evil as that, Melisande would have seen it in his heart. She never would have let him into our house or fed him our food."

And I remembered, suddenly, the way Mr. Jones had made Melisande smile by patting his belly at the end of the meal and remarking mournfully that the food was so good he hated to leave any behind. She'd fixed him a plate to take out to the wagon. I had a feeling I knew now who it had really been for. But to think of the tinker keeping this lad a prisoner inside the wagon just didn't make sense.

"Tell me the whole truth right now," I demanded. "Or I'll scream very loudly. Then you'll have even more explaining to do."

"They were dead," Harry said quickly, whether to prevent me from making good on my threat or because it was the only way he could get the information out, I couldn't quite tell. "Of the sweating sickness. No one else would take me, for fear that I had it as well. I did, in fact."

"So the tinker did you a great service," I said, not bothering to hide the outrage in my voice. "He saved your life. And to repay him for this kindness, you wish to steal his horse and run off."

"I do not want to be a tinker's boy!" Harry suddenly burst out. "I want to go back to the way things were! I—"

Without warning, his face seemed to crumple, for all that he was older than I was.

"I want a home," he whispered. "And they make fun of me in the towns. The other boys laugh and call me names. If I stay with the tinker, I'll never have any friends. I'd be better off on my own."

"You wouldn't, you know," I said quietly. "If you are different, it's better to have someone who cares for you, who looks out for you. It's better not to be alone."

"What would you know about it?" Harry said.

In answer, I let the shawl fall back from my head. Absolute stillness filled the barn. Not even the animals moved, or the dust motes in the shafts of moonlight.

"Did she do that to you?" Harry asked at last. "The sorceress?"

"Don't be ridiculous," I said. "She loves me. I don't know how it happened, as a matter of fact. It's just the way things are."

He took a step closer then, studying me as I'd studied him earlier. "How do you know?"

"How do I know what?"

"That she loves you," Harry replied.

"Because I asked her and she told me so," I answered. "And she always tells the truth. She has to, I think. It's related to her sorcery."

"Where are your parents?" Harry asked.

I shook my head. "I don't know. Melisande said my mother's heart had no room in it for me, and so she did the only thing she could: She made room inside her own. Perhaps it is the same with the tinker, did you stop to think of that? Maybe he's made room for you inside his heart. He might be sad if you went off and left him, and took his horse into the bargain."

"I doubt it," Harry said with a snort. "I'm not the easiest person to get along with."

"No, really?" I asked. And suddenly he smiled. He sat down on the floor and put his back against the door of the stall where I'd put the tinker's mare. She leaned over and lipped the top of his head.

"So we are both orphans, then, after a fashion," he said, as he reached up to stroke her long nose.

"I suppose we are," I acknowledged. I stood where I was for several more minutes, watching Harry with the horse, then went to sit on a bale of hay nearby.

"Does the tinker come this way often?" he asked, when I was seated.

"I have no idea," I said. "I never saw him until today, but we're hardly on the main road."

He kept his face angled downward, making it difficult to read his expression. "But if he did come back this way, he might stop, and you might be here?"

"We've lived here for as long as I can remember," I said. "We have no plans to leave, as far as I know."

"That might be all right, then," Harry said.

"It might be," I acknowledged. I stood up after a moment. "There's plenty of hay in the loft," I said. "Though I could get you a blanket, if you like."

"No, but I thank you," Harry said. "I'm sure hay will be enough."

"Good night, then, Harry," I said.

"Good night to you, Rapunzel. That means something, doesn't it?"

"It's a kind of parsley," I confessed. "To tell you the truth, it tastes pretty awful, but that's just my opinion."

He waited until I was all the way across the barn before he spoke again.

"What makes you so sure I won't steal the horse after you're gone?"

"Because you love her," I said. "And I have seen how much she loves the tinker. You can figure out the rest for yourself."

It wasn't until I was all the way back to the house that I realized my head was still bare, and I hadn't thought about it once.

FIVE

Harry stayed with the tinker, of course. In the years that followed—three of them, to be precise, until I turned sixteen and Harry a year or so older than that—as often as their ramblings permitted, the tinker and the young man stopped at our door. Mr. Jones liked to say he was calling upon his namesake, who had grown up sleek and fat and as copper as a penny and was the terror of every rodent for miles around.

The tinker himself grew slightly less ginger and somewhat more gray, while Harry shot up like a great weed that even I would have been able to recognize for what it was. For I had often heard Melisande say that it was the weeds that grew the strongest, the fastest, and the tallest, and Harry grew up both strong and tall.

His eyes, which I hadn't been able to see all that well in the barn that night, turned out to be a startling green, the same color as the leaves the apple trees put out in the springtime. His hair was the color of rich river mud. I never tired of reminding him of this second fact, just as he never tired of remarking in return that surely it was better to be blessed with even mud-colored hair than to be cursed with none.

We stared at each other, the first time he and the tinker returned. To tell you the truth, I don't think either of us truly expected to see the other again, for all the words that we had spoken. I'd thought of him often enough, though, and I wondered if he had thought of me. The two orphans.

"So, you are still here, Parsley."

As it happened, we were standing in the garden. After the great carrot disaster, Melisande had tried a new technique. Each row was clearly labeled with a little drawing of what the plant should look like, with its name written beneath. So far it seemed to be working. I was better both at their names and at pulling out what I was supposed to rather than what I was not.

"That was never much in doubt," I answered as tartly as I could. For the truth was, I was pleased to see him, but I knew it would never do to let him know this right off. "You were the one who was planning to steal a horse and run away, as I recall. And my name is Rapunzel."

"That's right. I remember now," he said. And then he flashed me a smile.

Oh ho, so that is the way of the world, I thought. For it seemed to me that, just beneath the skin of that smile, I could see the man that he would one day become. He was going to be a heartbreaker, at the rate he was going. I would have to make sure he didn't break mine.

"You came back," I said. "I wasn't all that certain that you would."

"Neither was I," he answered honestly. "But I kept remembering the things you'd said. Besides, I was curious." He shrugged.

"About what?"

"I thought maybe you'd grow some hair in my absence."

"I hate to disappoint you," I said, as I plucked off my garden hat to reveal the head underneath. "But I did not."

"I'm not disappointed," Harry said. "I brought something for you."

And it was only at that moment that I realized he'd been holding one hand behind his back.

"You brought me something?" I asked, astonished. So astonished that I forgot to put the hat back on my head.

"There's no need to get carried away," Harry said quickly, as if my reaction was cause for alarm. "It's just a piece of cloth. That's all."

He held it out, and I moved forward to take it from him.

He was right. It was, indeed, just a piece of cloth. But the cloth was the finest muslin I had ever seen, embroidered all over with gold-petaled flowers. They stood stiffly out from dark centers the exact same color as my eyes. The stitches were so fine and close, I could hardly see the muslin underneath.

"I know what these are," I said, and I couldn't have

kept the delight from my voice if I'd tried. "These are black-eyed Susans. They're my favorite flowers. How did you know?"

"What makes you think I did?" Harry asked. He began to stand first on one foot, and then the other, shifting his weight from side to side. "Maybe I just guessed and got it right, or chose it on a whim."

I looked up then, confused by his tone. He was sounding awfully surly and aggressive for someone offering a gift.

"It wouldn't matter if you had," I answered carefully but honestly. "I don't get gifts all that often."

He stood stock-still at this. "What's that supposed to mean?" he asked.

"Nothing," I said, beginning to get irritated in my turn. "It's just—there's only me and Melisande. She gives me a present on my birthday, of course, but until Mr. Jones gave me Mr. Jones . . ."

I let my voice run out. I was pretty sure I sounded ridiculous, and feared I might sound pathetic, which would have been much worse.

"I thought you might, you know, on your head," Harry said. "Even from here, I can hardly see the muslin. All you see is the gold, really, like—"

"Golden hair," I said. My chest felt tight and funny. I had never told anyone why I loved these particular flowers so much, not even Melisande. Their petals were the exact color I'd always dreamed my hair might be, assuming my head ever decided to cooperate and actually grow some.

"Thank you, Harry. It's lovely," I said.

He opened his mouth to make a smart remark, I was all but certain. He shut it with a snap, then tried a second time.

"You're welcome, Parsley," he said. "Don't you want to put it on?"

"Hold this," I said, and I handed him my gardening hat, then tied the kerchief on. It was soft and smooth against my head. "How does it look?"

He began to shift his weight again, as if his shoes were too tight in fits and starts. I gazed down at them, suddenly afraid to meet his eyes.

"How should I know? It looks all right."

"There's roast chicken and new potatoes for supper," I said. "With peas and mint, I think."

"Is there a pie?"

"A cherry pie," I said, looking back up. "I baked it just this morning."

Something came into his face then, a look that made me want to smile and weep all at the same time.

"My mother used to make cherry pies," he said. "They were my father's favorites."

"And yours?" I asked.

He nodded. "And mine."

"So we'd be even then," I said.

"We might be," he acknowledged. "Can I sleep in the hayloft? Mr. Jones snores."

"So does the cat," I said. And had the pleasure of hearing his quick laugh ring out.

"I can carry that," he said, extending a hand for the basket in which I'd carefully been placing lettuce leaves. I'd forgotten that I still had it over my arm. I held it back. I didn't need some boy carrying my things.

"So can I."

"I can do it better, though. I'm bigger and stronger. And I've seen more of the world than you have."

"What does that have to do with anything?"

"Parsley."

"Tinker's boy."

"Ah, so the two of you are making friends," a new voice said.

I turned to see Mr. Jones standing at the back door.

"Actually, we're already friends," I said, and was rewarded by the sound of Harry sucking in his breath. "We met once before."

"Is that so?" the tinker asked. His face stayed perfectly straight, but I could see the twinkle in the back of his eyes. *He's known all along about that first meeting,* I thought. And the only wonder was that Harry hadn't realized this long ago.

"Melisande says if you're quite finished, she would be pleased to have the lettuce you're supposed to be fetching in for supper."

"Here it is," Harry said. And, before I could prevent him, he snatched the basket right off my arm, then made a dash for the back door. With a laugh,

Mr. Jones scooted over quickly to avoid being flattened. That was when I saw it. Perhaps Melisande was right, and I had a gift for sorcery after all. For I'm sure that what I saw then was a quick and sudden glimpse into the tinker's heart.

I could see Harry, green eyes alight with mischief. And I thought I saw a girl as well. But she seemed far away, as if her place in Mr. Jones's heart was older than Harry's was. No less present, just not in front. For some reason I could neither see nor understand, she had been relegated to the background. I could not see her features clearly, but around her face, I thought I caught a glimpse of summer gold.

Not me, then, I thought.

And at the unexpected pang my own heart felt, my vision faltered, and Mr. Jones was just a man with graying ginger whiskers standing in an open door.

"Come in to dinner, Rapunzel," he said.

And so I did, and did not speak of what I had seen. For he had not asked me to look, and that which lies in another's heart, even if glimpsed out of turn, should never be told out of turn, if it can be helped.

SIX

I thought about it, though, from time to time. Who was the girl Mr. Jones kept at the back of his heart? Just as I wondered about the identity of the person Melisande kept hidden inside hers but never spoke of. *I made room for you inside my heart,* she'd told me on the day we first met Mr Jones. But who had she asked to scoot over so that I might have a place?

I did not ask either of these questions, though.

There are some subjects that, no matter how much your brain may tell you it would like an explanation, your heart and tongue refuse to touch. And so the question of who shared the sorceress's heart with me remained unanswered, because I could not bring myself to ask it.

And then it was forgotten, at least for a while.

For something changed the year I turned sixteen. A thing that at first seemed to have nothing to do with either Melisande or me, though it turned out to have a great deal to do with both of us.

It started out simply, with the weather. That summer was the hottest I could remember, the hottest I had ever known. For many weeks, too many, in fact, there had been no rain at all. Each day, early in the morning before the sun rose too high, Melisande and I labored together in the garden, carrying water from the stream that ran at the base of the apple orchard. Even then, our plants drooped and languished, as if they couldn't quite make up their minds to expend the energy required to stay alive.

It was the only time I ever saw the garden look anything other than rich and abundant. And if even Melisande's garden struggled as it did, I didn't want to think too long and hard about what might be happening to the gardens, and the people, in the town.

Some mornings, after our work was finished, I climbed to the top of the tallest apple tree, the one that grew at the very crest of the hill and so provided the best view of the surrounding countryside. This had been a favorite place for as long as I could remember. A place to sit and dream, to imagine where the roads I saw might go, or whether or not I might grow hair, and to watch for the arrival of Harry and Mr. Jones.

And so I was the first to notice the exodus from the city. One day the land was mostly empty, the next there were people, sometimes singly, sometimes in groups, moving in weary fits and starts down the thin brown snake of dusty road. Some toward the mountains, but most in the opposite direction, as if they wanted to put as great a distance between themselves and their misery as they could, in as short a time as possible.

Every once in a while, a single traveler would cut

across country and end up outside our back door. From them we heard tales of sickness in the city. Of a stillness of the air that was stifling the simplest breath and begetting a fever like none experienced before. Fear had come to live in the city, the travelers said, taking up more than its fair share of space and driving people from their homes. There were murmurs of some great evil magic at work in the land, the need to find its source and drive it out. Only then did I realize that most of those who came to us had known the way because they had been here before.

And so I came to understand their words for what they truly were: a warning.

The hot weather went on.

Several times I caught Melisande looking at me with that considering expression on her face, or standing perfectly still with her head cocked to one side, as if gauging the approach of something. The first time I saw this I felt my blood run as cold as our stream did all winter. *She is listening for the mob*, I thought.

But gradually I came to realize that it was something else. Which was not quite the same as saying we did not fear the mob would come. As the days passed and we still remained in our small house in the valley, I came to understand that Melisande was listening for the approach of Mr. Jones. It had to do with that very first conversation between them, I think, and of all that had not been spoken when the sorceress had told the tinker he would be welcome wherever we might dwell. We would wait for him now, or so it seemed, even with the risk of danger growing closer by the minute while, as far as I could hear, Mr. Jones did not.

One day, the day the radishes, the beans, and the spinach all expired at the exact same instant, I came to a decision of my own. I waited until the sorceress was busy in the house at the hottest part of the day, then I put my favorite kerchief on my head, the one that Harry had given me, with the black-eyed Susans embroidered upon it, and set off for the apple orchard. Not to climb my favorite tree, but to go beyond the orchard itself to the nearest farm.

The man who farmed the property closest to ours had always been a good neighbor, unconcerned and unafraid of sorcery. Once, several years ago now, he had come to Melisande in the middle of the night. His wife had gone into labor before her time. It was going badly, and he feared to leave her to make the journey to the town to fetch the midwife. And so, though she was no more skilled in childbirth than any other woman might be, Melisande had returned with him and done her best; by morning, the children had been born.

A boy and a girl, whom the farmer and his wife named William and Eleanor. They were small, for they had been born early, but they grew strong quickly. And they grew to be great squabblers, though they loved each other well, a fact of life that always made their father smile. It was the reason they had been born too soon, he said. They'd shared their mother's womb no more peaceably than they did their father's farmhouse.

The young boy, William, had a fondness for our apples. I often spied him in the orchard when the fruit was ripe. That time had not come yet, but I was hoping to catch a glimpse of William anyway, for I knew he liked to climb trees as much as I did. I found him in the second tallest tree in the orchard. My tree was the tallest, and that tree he never climbed.

"Come down, William," I said. "I want you to do an errand for me, if you will. Please go and fetch your father. I need to speak with him."

"What will you give me if I do?" the boy asked. In addition to squabbling, he also drove a hard bargain.

"I will give you this orchard for your very own," I replied. "Would you like that?"

"You can't," he said at once, but he did slide down out of the tree to stand beside me. "It doesn't belong to you. It belongs to the sorceress."

"What makes you think I would make such an offer without her permission?" I inquired, though in fact, I had not yet spoken to Melisande. The boy stood for a moment, staring at me with wide eyes. "Go fetch your father, William," I said again. "It's important."

Without another word, he turned and ran for home.

Before too many minutes had passed, I saw the farmer climbing swiftly up the hill. He was alone.

"Good day to you, Rapunzel," he said.

"Good day to you, Farmer Harris," I replied.

"My son has been telling me wild tales," the farmer said.

"Sooner or later, Melisande and I must leave this place," I said, seeing no reason not to come straight to the point. "You know what they have been saying in the town."

"I do," he nodded. He hesitated for a moment, as if uncertain whether to say any more. "I had thought, perhaps, to see you and the sorceress go before now."

I shook my head. "We will go when Melisande decides the time is right and not before. But I would not . . ." To my dismay, my voice faltered. Now that I had come to speak of it, the truth of what I was about to say struck hard. Very soon now, we would have to leave the only home that I had ever known.

"There's the livestock," I said. "And what's left of the crops. If the mob comes . . ."

"I know," the farmer said at once, and his face grew sober. "I know, Rapunzel."

"Would it not be a fine thing," I asked, "if both these farms were yours? One could be William's when he grows up. The other could be a dowry for your daughter."

"It might be a very fine thing," Farmer Harris said slowly. "It would be hard work until my son is grown, though."

"I cannot help with that," I said. "But perhaps, if the livestock were already in your own barn? They could be more easily cared for that way, I think. Except for the horse. We might need her for the journey."

"My wife's brother is young and strong," the farmer said, as if thinking it over. "He might come."

"That would be a great help," I said, at which he gave a quick smile.

"You have it all worked out, then?" he asked.

"No," I said. "Of course not. It's just—they'll drive us away," I burst out suddenly. "You know they will. I don't want everything we've cared for so well and for so long to belong to those who wish us ill. Not if I can help it."

"If they arrive before you are ready, come to me," the farmer said, and now his voice was strong and resolved. "My barn can hold more than extra livestock. On behalf of my son and daughter, I thank you for this kindness."

"I'll start bringing the animals tomorrow," I said.

And so we left one another.

I got home to find the sorceress standing at our back door.

"I've told Farmer Harris he can have the place when we leave it," I said. "I'll start taking over the first of the livestock tomorrow. If he already has them, it will be harder for others to take them away."

"That's good thinking," Melisande said quietly. "Thank you, Rapunzel." She made a gesture, the first I'd ever seen from her that looked anything like helplessness. "I meant to speak of this before now, but—"

"It doesn't matter," I interrupted swiftly. "As long as we both agree now."

"We agree," the sorceress said.

"So that's all right, then," I answered. "Now, what else needs to be done?"

Melisande's expression changed then, though I would be hard put to explain just how. It was as if I had answered a question for her, rather than asked one of her. And the answer had settled things, once and for all.

"We should decide what we want to take with us," she said. "And have it ready, for we may have to go at a moment's notice."

"That is easily done," I replied. "For there's not much I want, save for you and the cat, and this kerchief, but I usually have it on."

"Life is very simple, then," Melisande agreed. "For as long as you are with me, I am satisfied."

"A little food and water might be a good idea, though," I said, amazed to feel myself starting to smile. I might share her heart, but for the moment it seemed that I alone was all that she required.

"Oh, indeed," the sorceress replied.

In the days that followed, we set about doing what needed to be done. By the end of that week, all our livestock—the goats, the cow, the sheep and the pigs—had been walked across the fields to the Harris farm. The belongings Melisande and I planned to take with us were tied in two large shawls, which sat in readiness by the front door. Melisande's sewing basket, which had a hinged lid, stood ready to carry the cat. I spent many moments explaining this future indignity to him, promising that it was absolutely necessary and would be as short-lived as possible.

And still the weather stayed hot, and the tinker and his boy did not come.

SEVEN

Eventually, of course, the matter was taken out of our hands, for that is the way of things, more often than not. Returning from the orchard late one day, where I had been battling wasps for apples that the heat had brought down before their time, I saw a great cloud of dust. From the hill on which the orchard stood, I could trace the cloud's path with my eyes: from the main road, off onto the several branching ones that, eventually, led to our front door.

No! I thought. It would be bad enough for the mob to catch us at all, but for them to find Melisande alone . . .

Without another thought in my head, I sprinted for home.

Halfway there, my brain kicked in, reminding me that if I simply burst in upon whatever I might find, not only would I be unable to aid the sorceress, I'd hand myself over to our enemies as well. So I stopped, set the basket of apples down, and took a breath. Then, leaving the basket where it was, I continued more slowly.

There was no one in the garden. The back door was shut, and I could hear no sound from inside the house. In the whole yard, there seemed to be not a single breath of air. The back of my neck prickled with tension. I crept around to the front and found a horse standing in our yard. Its flanks were covered with sweat. White foam flecked its mouth. I stood for a moment, while my own sweat dampened the back of my dress, trying to decide what should be done. Unless cared for, a horse ridden as hard as this one could sicken.

I suppose there's nothing for it, I thought, as I took a single step forward. If its master had evil intentions, the horse would suffer quite enough without my adding to its misery.

"Don't you touch him. Stay away," a shrill voice called.

Instantly I took the same step back, cursing myself. I'd let my love for animals get in the way of my good sense. Again.

"I only want to wipe him down," I said. "He shouldn't be left to stand. He's been ridden too hard."

"I said stay away," the voice said again, and now I could see to whom it belonged. In the lane right outside our gate sat a serving boy on a horse of his own. The lad was big and strapping, for all that his voice had been shrill. He had ears like pitchers. Great, doughy hands clutched hard at the reins so that the horse's feet were never still. It tossed its head and showed the whites of its eyes.

He is infected by his rider's fear, I thought.

"I only want to wipe him down," I said again.

"And I can bring you a drink of water, if you like."

"You'll do no such thing," the boy replied. "How do I know what you might put in it? You serve the evil sorceress."

"I do not," I answered smartly, probably more smartly than I should have done. But that word, evil, was pounding in my head, driving out caution. "I'm nobody's servant, and if you think that Melisande would harm anyone, you're just plain wrong. Maybe you should consider keeping your mouth shut. Your ignorance is showing, and it's not a pretty sight."

"What would you know about pretty?" the boy shot back. "I've heard about you. They say that you are cursed and have no hair at all."

"That's ridiculous," I said, though I was responding to the first part of his words, of course. My voice was loud and brave, but by now my heart had begun to knock against my ribs. What was I doing, standing here arguing in the yard?

"Show me your head and prove it, then," the boy challenged, for of course I had a kerchief on, as always, and my favorite one besides.

"I don't have to prove anything to you," I said. At which he laughed, and it was not a joyful sound.

"You're afraid of me," he said. "You ought to be."

All of a sudden, I understood the urge to strike the first blow, to harm those you think mean to injure you before they get the chance. For his words made me angry, and my fingers itched to find a rock and throw it. But before I could do anything so rash—

before, in fact, I could do anything else at all—the front door of the house slammed back and a man stalked out into the yard. I spun toward him. He stopped short. We stared at one another.

He was a few years older than I was, or so I judged, dressed in the fine clothes of a wealthy man from the town. A merchant, perhaps. They always dressed well.

"So," he said at last. "You have grown up tall. I wondered if you might, your legs were so strong."

I did my best to hide my confusion, but I must not have been very successful.

"You don't remember me, do you?" he inquired.

I opened my mouth to say that of course I didn't, when I looked into his eyes. They were a color I had seen just once before, a blue more blue than any sky. In that moment, a memory I had forgotten I possessed returned to me, and I discovered that I knew him after all.

"You are the boy," I said. "The tall boy who kicked the ball so well."

He smiled then, and it was like the sun appearing on a cloudy day, just when you have given up any hope that such a moment might come.

"And you are the girl who was faster than any of us," he said. He made a gesture, as if both calling attention to and dismissing the rich garments that he wore. "As you can see, we have both grown up."

"You have done well," I said.

He shrugged. "My father died young and I am his

only son. But I . . ." He paused and took a breath. "I have never forgotten the day we met."

The things you saw in your own heart, I thought. But I did not say so aloud. For this I did remember clearly: Not even he had been able to hold Melisande's eyes.

"And so I came to offer you and the sorceress this warning: Leave this place with all possible speed, or you will answer with your lives."

I exhaled a breath I hadn't realized I'd been holding in.

"You came to warn us," I said. "Not to drive us off."

"The first will accomplish the second, so I'm not sure it makes much difference," he said. "But no, I did not come to drive you off. I failed to defend you once. I would prefer not to make the same mistake a second time. Consider this the payment of a debt."

He moved then, striding across the yard to mount his horse. Then, for one moment only, he looked down.

"I do not think that we will meet again. Go quickly, and fare you well."

Then he spurred his horse back into the lane and vanished down it in the same cloud of dust with which he had arrived. But the serving boy, freed from his master's presence and his fear alike, was not quite done. With a great cry, he aimed his horse through the gate, straight at me, acting so quickly I had no time to step aside. With one fierce gesture, he yanked the kerchief from my head.

"I knew it! I knew it! You *are* cursed!" he cried.

With a final flourish, he tossed the fabric high into the air, then sped after his master, the horse's legs eating up the road. And it was only then that I turned and saw Harry, standing at the corner of the house. In one white-knuckled fist, he clutched the tallest of our pitchforks.

Slowly I crossed the yard, retrieved my kerchief, shook it out, and put it back on. I did my best to keep my spine straight, like the stems of the black-eyed Susans that I so loved. Only then did I realize what strength it took to stand up so tall and straight and unafraid, no matter what comes.

"I'm sorry, Rapunzel," Harry said.

"You didn't do anything," I said. "You don't have anything to be sorry for."

"Don't I?" Harry asked. "Thank you for reminding me." And he came forward then, taking several steps and driving the pitchfork, hard, into the parched ground.

"What are you talking about?" I asked. Every bone in my body seemed to ache, all of a sudden. Even my brain ached, for it felt worn out and tired.

"How can you ask me that?" Harry cried. "I just stood there. I stood there while he hurt you and did nothing. It was over before I knew what should be done."

"He didn't hurt me," I said.

"Of course he did. Why else are you crying?"

And it was only as he said this that I realized it was the truth. My dusty cheeks were wet with tears.

"I'm crying because I'm angry, not hurt," I said as I dashed them aside. "The wound he wanted to inflict was over and done with long ago. We've done nothing to them. Nothing! But still they'll come to drive us from our home. All because we're diffcrent, and they are fearful fools who require a scapegoat. Where's Melisande?"

"Here," I heard the sorceress call.

She stepped out into the yard. On her back she had tied her own bundle. She set mine down at her feet. Her sewing basket rested in the crook of one arm.

"The cat and I have been coming to an arrangement," she said. "He agrees not to scratch or cry out, if we agree to keep him in this basket for as short a time as possible."

"I'm glad you had better luck convincing him than I did," I said. I moved to her side and shouldered my own bundle. She handed over the basket containing Mr. Jones, then went back inside for the one in which we'd packed our food supplies. Then she came all the way out and shut the door behind her.

"Harry," she said, precisely as if she had expected to see him there on this afternoon and no other. "There you are."

"The tinker is at the next farm over," Harry said. "He said that you would know the one. And he said you should go quickly to join him. There isn't much time."

"I know," said Melisande.

"What are you going to do?" I asked him. For there had been a note in his voice, one I wasn't certain that I liked.

"I've been thinking about that," Harry said. "I'm taking the horse."

"Oh, no, you're not," I said. "He's coming with us."

"No," Harry said at once, and his eyes went to Melisande's as if seeking support. "Surely you can see that isn't wise. It's well enough known that the tinker stops at your door. If he's seen on the road with your horse . . ."

"But . . . ," I said.

"Harry is right," Melisande spoke up. "If we are to ride with the tinker, we cannot afford to give anyone cause to search the wagon."

"If anyone asks, I can always say that I stole it," Harry went on. "I can travel fast and light, and meet up with you later."

"In that case," I said tartly, "I sincerely hope one of us knows where we're going."

"Across the mountains," Melisande said. "Three days' journey through the passes, two days across the plains beyond. On the morning of the sixth day, look for a tower rising straight up out of the plain. That is where we are going."

"Why?" I asked.

But the sorceress shook her head. "Not now. There will be time enough for that when we are safely away from this place." She turned to go, then paused, her eyes on Harry. "Say your good-byes quickly. I'll wait for you at the top of the hill, Rapunzel."

With that, she turned on one heel and disappeared around the side of the house, leaving Harry and me standing in the yard.

"Six days," Harry said. "That's not so bad. Surely even you can stay out of trouble for that long, Parsley."

"I am never any trouble," I retorted. "That falls to horse-stealing tinker's boys."

But I moved to him and reached for his hand before I quite knew what I had done.

"Be careful," I said. "I want you to promise."

"You're the one they're hunting, not me," he said.

"Harry."

"Oh, all right. I promise, Parsley."

"Why must you always do that?" I asked, horrified that I could once more feel the prick of tears at the back of my eyes, and I knew that anger hadn't brought them on this time. I stamped my foot, to drive them away. "I have a proper name. You might learn to say it."

"Rapunzel," Harry said. And again, "Rapunzel."

And then he did the very last thing I expected. He caught my face between his hands and pressed his lips to mine. I forgot the heat of the day, forgot my own danger. All I could feel was the touch of his mouth. All I could hear was the sound my own heart made.

Home, it said. *Home*.

Then, quickly as it had arrived, the moment was over. He let me go, stepped back, and spun me around.

"Now, run, Parsley. If I find out you've let them catch you, I'll hunt you down and tar and feather you myself."

I did run then, all the way to the crest of the hill, where the sorceress was waiting beneath my favorite apple tree. Then, just once and only for a moment, I stopped and turned around.

The house sat just where it always had, and beyond it the barn. But of our horse, with the tinker's boy upon its back, I could see no sign. Melisande reached out and put a hand on my arm.

"I know," I said. "I know."

And so, together, we turned away and hurried down the far side of the hill.

But to the end of my days, my heart retained this picture: an image of the black-eyed Susans standing tall and straight and true in the ruins of our abandoned garden.

EIGHT

Our journey went just as the sorceress had said it would. Three days through the mountain passes, two days across the plains beyond. We stayed inside the wagon all the first three days, until we reached a place where the mountains ended suddenly, as if cut off with a knife, and a wide, flat plain stretched out in every direction, eventually becoming the horizon line.

It was hot and stuffy in the wagon. All four sides were down, lashed tight, in spite of the fact that it was summer and the weather was warm. My body ached from the inactivity. I had never been so restricted before, never even thought about what it might be like to be unable to do something as simple as taking a few steps. To be unable to feel the wind or see the sky. I would rouse from sudden stupors to find my hands had clenched themselves into fists, as if I had dreamed fierce dreams while I dozed.

None of us spoke very much.

At night the tinker sat beside his fire and conversed with those who stopped to share its light. But they were few, though the road held travelers other than ourselves. It was as if all were infected by the

73

sickness that had struck the town. Not the fever, but the sickness of suspicion. Fear walked that road, planting its feet as solidly as those of Mr. Jones's horse.

And so the first three days passed slowly, until, at last, we left the mountains behind.

Free of the mountains, the land opened up like a child suddenly freed of a heavy winter coat, gleefully spreading its arms. The road we traveled upon opened up also, becoming wide and broad. There was a flash of light off to the west. Somewhere in the distance, a river flowed. It was cooler on the far side of the mountains, as if the heat that had held us in so tight a grip had hands but no legs and so had been unable to make the climb. About mid-morning on the fourth day, Mr. Jones brought the horse and wagon to a sudden halt. A moment later he poked his head through the opening at his back.

"I have seen no other people for a good two hours," he said. "I think it's safe for you to come out now."

"You go first, Rapunzel," Melisande said. "Perhaps it will still be better if we don't both suddenly appear at once."

I wish I could tell you that at this moment I was overcome by a fit of thoughtfulness. That I turned to the woman who had raised me and said, "Oh, no, Melisande. You go first. You've been just as cramped and miserable as I."

I didn't, though.

Instead, I scrambled for the front of the wagon without another word, almost tumbling over the seat and onto the horse's back in my eagerness to reach the outside.

"Take it easy," Mr. Jones said. "The world's not going anywhere, you know."

"I don't know that, as a matter of fact," I said.

And then I did what I had started to do three days ago and hadn't finished yet. I began to run.

I ran until my legs ached just as much with exertion as they had with inertia. Until the breath scorched going down my parched throat and burned inside my lungs. Until the kerchief I wore was plastered to my head with sweat, and then the sweat dripped down into my eyes. I ran until my hands hung limply, too worn out to make fists at my sides. And then I stopped and caught my breath, and sat down to wait by the side of the road.

By the time the wagon pulled up beside me, Melisande was sitting next to Mr. Jones.

"You ran a long way," she said. "Was it far enough?"

"I'm not sure I know."

"You'll appreciate a drink of water, in any case," the tinker said.

"I would," I acknowledged. "And a change of head-gear, I think."

"Fortunately for you, I believe I can assist with both." He handed over the waterskin, then climbed down from the seat of the wagon and began to rummage in the wagon itself. The sides had been rolled up, I noticed. Our hiding place was now completely gone.

"Harry found this, our last trip together," the tinker said, and he handed me what my fingers told me was yet another piece of cloth, even as my eyes watched it flash in the sun. "He intended to give it to you himself, of course."

After that first gift of cloth for a kerchief, Harry had continued to bring me such presents from time to time. Each more elaborate and fanciful than the next, till even Melisande looked forward to seeing what would arrive. Some were shot through with threads of gold and silver. Others were woven of every color I could imagine, and even some that I could not. The most recent had been stitched to resemble a peacock's tail, with actual feathers fluttering along its edges. We'd put that one on the head of the scarecrow in the cornfield, where it had successfully intimidated the crows.

I held the fabric by one corner and let the rest flutter out in the breeze.

"For heaven's sake, I can't wear this!" I exclaimed. "I'll blind the horse."

"You might at that," Mr. Jones agreed. For, rather than being covered only with embroidery, this cloth was decorated with tiny mirrors held in place with elaborate stitches in red and silver. "It's very beautiful, though. I can see why Harry thought you might like it."

"Harry," I said, and tried not to hear the way my voice threatened to turn those two syllables into a sob.

"He'll be all right, Rapunzel," the tinker said. "He's young and strong, and he knows the roads."

"Of course he'll be all right," I said, as if I could hide my fears by the crossness in my voice. "It's just so like him to be late."

"He's not late yet," said Melisande. Then, to my surprise, she hopped down from the wagon seat. "Here," she said. "You ride and I'll run for a while. By nightfall we will come to a place where the river turns to run beside the road. There is a small stand of trees where the river bends that makes a fine campsite. There I will answer all the questions you've been so careful not to ask. For which I am most grateful, by the way."

"Can I have a bath?" I inquired.

"Yes," the sorceress answered, and she smiled. "That question I can answer now."

"I heard what he said to you," Melisande said, late that night. "The boy, that last day, in our yard. He said that you were cursed. Not only is this cruel and unfair, it's also untrue. For it is not you who is cursed, my Rapunzel. It is I."

We had come to the bend in the river, just as the sorceress had declared we would. Made camp, eaten our dinner, and washed from our bodies the stains that fear makes, and the dust from the road. Now the three of us sat around a small, bright campfire, while Mr. Jones's horse grazed nearby.

The tinker had brought out a pipe, and its bowl illuminated his face, then darkened it again, as he puffed. Its fragrant smoke mingled with the smoke of the fire. The water beside us made a cheerful sound. I was grateful for this, for I had found to my surprise that the land made me nervous in the darkness. It was so great and open and wide. In it, Melisande's words seemed to fly out in every direction, gone almost before I could understand what she had said.

"How can that be?" I asked. "Who has the power to curse a sorceress?"

"The answer to that is simple," the sorceress herself replied. "One whose power is greater than mine. In this case, it was a wizard, and for this reason: He had witnessed me doing a thing that I should not have done. Once, a very long time ago now, I committed an act of unkindness."

"But," I said, then stopped short. Who was I to question the actions of a wizard, after all? But Melisande seemed to understand what my objection might have been, had I decided to say it aloud.

"True enough," she acknowledged. "Acts of unkindness happen every day, some intentional, others not. Mine was of the second variety, not that it made any difference in the long run."

"I'm not sure I understand," I said.

"That is not surprising," Melisande answered. "For it has taken many years for me to understand it myself."

She fell silent for a moment, gazing into the fire, then lifted her eyes to mine. When she did, I got a jolt. For it seemed to me that, just as I had done with the tinker on that day so long ago now, I caught a glimpse into the sorceress's heart. In it I thought I recognized myself. But behind me, moving closer even as I watched, was the person Melisande had asked to step aside. Though for many years we had not discussed how I had first come to live with her, I had never forgotten her words: *I made room for you inside my heart.*

It is another girl, I realized. Just as I thought she might come close enough for me to see her features, Melisande spoke again, and the vision vanished.

"I have wanted to tell you this story many times, Rapunzel," she said. "Even more, I have known that I must. But every time I wondered if the time was right, my heart counseled me to wait, and I listened to its voice. For that is supposed to be my gift, is it not? To see what is in the heart?"

"In another's heart, yes," I answered without thinking, for my head was still full of what I believed I had seen, trying to figure it out. Mr. Jones shifted position suddenly, as if he would have answered differently if the question had been put to him. But the sorceress simply nodded.

"That is a just response. To see into another's

heart is one thing. To see into one's own heart may require a different power entirely. I'm still not entirely certain it's one that I possess."

And so the sorceress told us her story.

NINE

"Many years ago," Melisande said, "long before you were born, Rapunzel, the world was less afraid of magic than it is now. As a result, magic itself was more powerful. In this, I suppose it could be said that it was like a radish in our garden."

"Better that than a carrot," I said, and heard both the tinker and the sorceress chuckle. And with that, I felt the tension around our fire ease, as if, now that the story had at last commenced, we all understood we would stick with it till the close. What might happen then was anyone's guess, but for now, we would all be united in the telling and hearing of it.

"Though it could be any plant," I went on, "assuming that I've grasped your point. If you give a plant room, it will grow and flourish. But if you crowd it, you may choke it out."

"That is indeed my point," Melisande agreed. "Not that magic has died out entirely in these days. But fear is strong. Fear of what is different, of what cannot easily be explained, particularly explained away. We've had proof enough of that recently, I think, you and I."

"But this is not a story of these days," I said.

"No," Melisande agreed. "Or at least, the start of it is not, for this story is still ongoing. It has not yet come to its conclusion, though I hope that the day for that is not far off. It is a cautionary tale, one that shows how, even when used with the best intentions, the strongest magic can still go wrong.

"Like many such tales, it began innocently enough. One fine market day, a sorceress and her daughter, who was just the age that you are now, Rapunzel, left their home and went to the nearest town."

"Wait a minute. Stop right there," I said. I felt a shock, as if I had suddenly been plunged into cold, deep water. "You have a daughter. A daughter of your own blood."

"I do," answered Melisande. "Her father and I were childhood sweethearts. He died long ago. My daughter was once all that I had in the world."

I opened my mouth, then closed it, then opened it again, and still no sound came out. The numbness of shock was being replaced by a strange sensation, tingling in all my limbs as if my entire being was undergoing some great rearrangement of its very essence. All these years the sorceress had had a child, a daughter who was all she had in the world, yet not once had she ever spoken of her.

"What is her name?" the tinker asked quietly.

"I do not speak the name I gave her at her birth," Melisande answered, matching his tone. "She lost it the same day as the events I am about to tell. For many years now, she has been called Rue. She dwells in the tower we will reach in another day's time."

Rue, I thought. Another plant in the garden. A name even more bitter than mine. Rue for sorrow. Rue for regret.

"What a terrible thing to be called," I said aloud, before I quite realized I had done so.

"I understand this must be difficult for you," Melisande began.

"Oh, do you?" I burst out. "I don't think you understand anything at all. I know I don't."

How could you? I wanted to cry. *How can you say you love me and hold something like this back?*

It did no good for my mind to insist that the sorceress had always told me the truth. She had not told me of her own, her other, child. An omission so large and strange that, in that moment, it felt no different than the telling of a lie.

"Let her finish, Rapunzel," Mr. Jones said, his own voice calm. "There can be time for pain and outrage later, if that is still what you feel. But we'll never get anywhere if you indulge in them now."

Almost, I did it. Stood up and left the fire. Almost, I walked off into that great, vast darkness that surrounded us. Walked off and kept on going. For it didn't seem like such a foreign country now. In the moments since the sorceress had revealed that she had a daughter, vast and dark and empty had become familiar territory. It was just the same as the inside of my heart.

I didn't move, though. Instead I took hold of my pain and throttled it down. *Mr. Jones is right*, I thought. There would be time for pain and outrage later. Later I could scream and weep to my certainly confused and maybe even broken heart's content. For the moment, however, only by being silent could I learn what I needed to know.

"I'm sorry," I said. "Please, go on."

"I'm sorry too," answered Melisande. "More sorry than you know. And so I will begin with two unkindnesses, it seems. One, tonight. The first, long ago."

"Upon a market day, you said," I prompted, suddenly eager to get the telling of this tale over and done with. "You took *me* to town upon a market day also, as I recall."

"I did," said Melisande. "And though what happened brought you pain, it also showed me that your heart was strong. Stronger than you knew then. Perhaps it is still stronger than you know."

"So it was a test, then?" I asked, as the pain and confusion I was trying to master grew too strong and slipped their hold. Was my childhood nothing but a series of hidden checks and balances, not really what I thought I had experienced at all?

"How fortunate for us that I passed it," I went on, unable to keep the bitterness from my voice. "How many more are there to be, or don't I get to know until they're all over?"

"Enough, Rapunzel," Mr. Jones said. I shut my mouth with a snap and pressed the tip of my tongue against the back of my teeth. "Let the sorceress tell what must be told."

"Upon a market day, as I have said," Melisande resumed her tale, "my daughter and I went to town. There she saw a bright ribbon for her hair. She had eyes for nothing else. I had eyes for no one but my child. On that day, I, whose gift it is to see into the hearts of others, failed to see that my daughter's heart was not the only one filled with desire. She had that ribbon for her hair, while another woman's child had none."

"Oh, but surely—" I began to protest, then stopped. We were never going to get anywhere if I kept interrupting every other sentence. Not only that, I was contradicting myself. A moment ago I had been ready to use my words to lash out. Now here I was, jumping to Melisande's defense.

"You are exactly right," she said at once, precisely as if she understood the objection I had planned to make.

"The act was simple and unintentional, not deliberately cruel, but merely thoughtless. I thought only of myself and what I loved. Everyday people do this all the time, though I suppose it could be said the world might be a better place if they did not. But I am not an everyday sort of person. I possess a gift, the gift to see what lies inside another's heart.

"On that day, I did not look. I let myself be blind. It was this fact more than any other that weighed against me in the end. That made the wizard who saw my actions decide I needed to be taught a lesson in the uses of power."

"But *why?*" I cried.

"My gift is not simply a skill I *may* use, it is a skill I *must* use," Melisande replied. "Not that I am required to act on what my eyes discover. My gift, my responsibility, is to see and nothing more. I am free to choose my own actions. Indeed, like everyone else, I must be so. A good act that is compelled is not goodness at all, but merely force.

"It might even have been better if I had been deliberately unkind. A will to be unkind is like a sickness. It can be healed or driven out. But to be unkind because you are thoughtless is the worst kind of blindness: difficult to cure, because you cannot see the fault even as you commit it."

"And that's why the wizard put a curse on you?" I asked.

"It is," Melisande replied. "Because I failed to look for what another held in her heart, I would be unable to see what I held in mine, for a time. It would not wither. It would not fade away. But neither would it grow. It would remain just as it was, as if in a dream of life, until I found the means to awaken it and set it free."

"What is it about wizards?" Mr. Jones remarked. "They expend so much effort to say so little."

"I couldn't agree more," Melisande replied, with a slight smile. "If the wizard had been less fond of the sound of his own voice, he might have realized he was making a mistake of his own. Power was what he held most closely in his own heart, so he assumed it was the same for mine. He therefore hoped to teach me a lesson in the uses of power by depriving me of it. Instead he deprived me of a thing I loved much more."

"Your daughter," I said suddenly, and felt my pain and anger begin to drain away and be replaced by something else, though I wasn't sure quite what.

"My daughter," Melisande echoed quietly. "The wizard did not mean his curse to touch my child, any more than I meant to be unkind to the child of another. But, like my own thoughtless action, once the wizard's curse was uttered, it could not be undone. And so I kept sight of my power, but lost sight of the thing I valued most: my child.

"The wizard took her and placed her in a tower he used his magic to build in two nights and the day that fell between them. It is made of smooth, gray stone. Windows made of starlight ring the top. Its door may be seen and opened only by the power of a love other than my own. There my child has stayed from that day to this, waiting for me to bring the key, the means of awakening and freeing her heart."

"You think it's me," I said. By now I felt so many different things, I was well on my way to deciding it might be preferable to feel nothing. "That's the real reason you took me in and raised me. You need me to free your daughter. You don't love me at all."

"That's not true," Melisande said at once. "I took

you in and raised you for the same reason I have always said: Because I loved you from the moment I first saw you, Rapunzel. But I will admit that there is more. When I gazed into your mother's heart and found no room for you within it, I heard a sound, like the opening of a door. It seemed to me that her inability to look with the eyes of love could not be coincidence. At long last, perhaps I was being offered the chance to redeem the daughter I had lost.

"But only if I could take you in and love you truly, if I could teach you all the things my heart had learned in the days since Rue had been taken and locked away. And so I did what the woman who gave birth to you could not. I looked with the eyes of love, claimed you, and raised you as my own."

"And never mentioned your daughter once," I added, finishing the list. "Until tonight, when I'm supposed to meet her tomorrow. Is this my final test? What happens if we can't stand the sight of one another?"

"I don't know," Melisande said, her own voice rising for the very first time. "I can't see the future. That is not my gift. I don't know what is to come. I've done what I thought was right, what I thought I must. That's all I can tell you."

"What about what I want to do?" I asked. "Suppose all I want to do is turn around and go back home? Does what I want even matter? Do I have a choice?"

"Of course you have a choice," Mr. Jones said, his

first words for what seemed like a very long time. "The sorceress has said what she has done, but she cannot say what you will do. That, only you can decide."

"Thank you," I said. "I'm glad to see somebody's on my side."

Mr. Jones knocked his pipe out on a stone without looking up. "It is not a matter of taking sides. It is what it has always been: a matter of the heart. You may think you are listening, but you're hearing only what you want to hear, Rapunzel. What is in the heart cannot be forced. This, the sorceress has already acknowledged. If the heart bends, it must be of its own free will, or not at all.

"Personally, I think she's right. Your heart is stronger than you know. But you may never learn how strong unless you put it to the test."

"I'm tired of being tested," I replied.

"Now that," the tinker said briskly, as he got to his feet, "is a feeling I understand very well. I'm sorry to tell you that it may not make much difference in the long run, though." He came over and kissed me on the cheek, an action he had never performed before. "I suggest we all go to sleep. I don't know about anyone else, but I am tired. I'd put an extra blanket on if I were you, Rapunzel. Even summer nights on the plain are cold."

With that, he moved to the wagon, pulled his own bedroll from it, and went to bed down close to the horse. I went to lie in my usual position, wrapping myself in an extra blanket as the tinker had suggested, my arms around my knees as if to make myself as small as possible. For the first and only time that I could remember, Melisande and I did not say good night.

All through that night, the sorceress stayed beside the fire. What her thoughts were, as the fire died down to nothing more than cold gray ash, I cannot say. To the best of my knowledge, she never told another living soul.

TEN

I did not go back home in the end, of course.

You've heard the saying, better the devil you know than the one you do not? What a load of poppycock. In fact, if I had to make a guess, it would be that whoever came up with that particular phrase was never called upon to face any sort of devil in his or her life.

What did I have to go back for, after all? I'd only be going right back into danger, the very same danger I'd just gone to such great lengths to avoid. It was hardly as if there would be anyone at the end of the road, or even anywhere along it, waiting to welcome me with open arms.

It wasn't all that likely there would be open arms if I went forward, either, but at least I would be going into the unknown. And here is a fact of life that those who are quick to speak of devils never mention: As long as a thing is unknown, it belongs to us in a way that well-known things do not. For we have the opportunity to fill the empty, unknown spaces for ourselves, and in them there is room for imagination and for hope.

If I went forward, I might imagine that I could

somehow pass this impossible test. Maybe my heart *was* stronger than I knew, and all would yet be well. So, on the morning of the fifth day, going forward was precisely what I did. On the morning of the sixth day, I saw Rue's tower for the very first time.

I might have guessed there was some magic at work in its construction, even if I had not been told this ahead of time. Surely any sort of structure should have been visible for miles away in that flat land. Instead, you could see the tower clearly only when you had actually arrived. It rose up out of the ground like a great tree trunk of hard, gray stone, its roots indistinguishable from the very bones of the earth itself.

The tower the wizard had created to house the innocent victim of his curse was perfectly cylindrical, perfectly smooth. I could neither see nor feel one seam or chink to show that the stone had ever been cut. At what I thought of as the tower's back, though this was merely my own fancy as a circle has no such thing, was the river. A dense forest held it in a great, green embrace on its other three sides. All around, just as wide as two carts abreast, ran a close-cropped greensward.

If I leaned back and shaded my eyes, I could see a wrought-iron railing, intricately carved, running around the tower's very top. Just behind it, a circle of windows caught the light. But no matter how many times I walked around it, three to be precise, I could find no sign of any door. At the end of my third circuit

I stopped beside the sorceress and said, "How do we get up? I assume that's what you have in mind."

Conversation between us was still stilted, at best. Among all of us, if it came to that. Even Mr. Jones had kept silent during the last day of our journey, as if wrapped in his own thoughts. Not that there was much use in talking. It would be deeds, not words, that would end the story and decide its outcome.

While I walked around the tower and Melisande stood perfectly still, Mr. Jones unhitched the horse and let her wade into the river, which here was broad and shallow. As if he had no other care in the world, the tinker washed clothes at the river's edge, then spread them out to dry. I knew what he was doing, of course. He was letting the sorceress and me sort things out on our own. Mr. Jones was hidden now by the bulk of the tower, for Melisande and I stood with our backs to the forest, and the river was on the other side, out of sight.

"More wizardry," Melisande replied now. "There's a password of sorts. Rapunzel, I—"

"I really wish you wouldn't," I interrupted swiftly, suddenly afraid that I might cry. I was trying to do what Melisande herself had done—what I thought was right, what I thought I must. But I was still hurt and uncertain, and more than a little afraid. If we stood around talking about it for very much longer, chances were good I'd lose my nerve entirely.

"By my own free will, I shall go up," I said. "But I cannot promise I'll be willing to stay, not from down here, anyhow. Your daughter and I must decide that together, I think."

"Fair enough," said Melisande.

I pulled in what felt too much like my last breath of free air. "Okay," I said. "I'm ready whenever you are."

Melisande took a deep breath of her own, as if steeling herself. Then, in a loud, firm voice, she pronounced the following words:

"One so fair, let down your hair. Let me go from here to there."

What on earth? I thought.

For many moments nothing seemed to happen, unless you count the fact that my heart suddenly began to pound. Then, with a start, I realized that the tower was changing before my eyes. No longer did the stone look dull and gray. Instead it seemed to flush. Veins of color suddenly appeared, spreading upward, branching out as blood runs through a body. They shimmered as they caught the light.

It looks alive, I thought. As if the tower had been sleeping as bears do in the winter, and Melisande's words were the harbingers of spring, the wake-up call.

Together, the sorceress and I watched the flush of color rise all the way to the tower's top. Then, with a sound like a flock of birds all launching themselves into the air at once, a single pane of glass flew back, and a thick woven rope came flying out. It wrapped itself twice around the iron railing, as if it wished to anchor itself more firmly, then plummeted straight over the side to land at our feet with a soft *plunk*.

It was the most beautiful golden color that I had ever seen. Braided tightly together, almost too thick for my hands to close around. At its end was tied a ribbon of so dark a red it was almost black. *Heart's blood*, I thought. And in that moment, I thought I understood, and could have sworn I felt my own heart stop.

This wizardry is a terrible thing, I thought.

Then Melisande reached for the golden braid, and I saw that her hand trembled for the one and only time in all the years that I had known her. At this, my heart gave a great jolt of pity within my breast, then began to beat in its normal way once more. But before Melisande could take hold of the braid, a streak of copper caught my eye. Running as hard as he could, Mr. Jones, the cat, streaked around the side of the tower, gave a great leap with all four legs outstretched, landed upon the golden braid, and began to scramble upward. Halfway up the tower he stopped and seemed to glance back at us over one furry shoulder.

What are you waiting for? his expression inquired. Clearly, this was the most exciting adventure in the world, and only a fool would decline to be a part of it.

"After you," I said. Melisande's fingers wrapped around the golden braid. We began to climb upward in single file.

It was hard work. Much harder than it looked, particularly if one judged by the cat. The braid was thick and soft, difficult to hold. More than once I had the feeling that, if I loosened my grip for even a second, the braid would slip right through my hands and I'd tumble to the ground. Several times I wished for Mr. Jones's claws. Not only that, the braid wouldn't stay still. No kind of rope ladder ever does, I suppose. Melisande's exertions pulled it one way, while mine pulled it another. Slowly, we made our precarious and strenuous way up the side of the tower.

Eventually I felt the braid give a great jerk. I looked up, startled, just in time to see Melisande throw one foot over the iron railing. In the next moment, she had disappeared over its side. Then her head reappeared, and she reached down and helped to pull me up after her. I tumbled over the railing in a great ungainly heap, then lay flat on my back, on a wide shelf of stone at the tower's top. After a few moments, Mr. Jones came over and sat upon my chest, gazing down at me with pleased and excited eyes.

"Show-off," I muttered. "It's considered impolite to gloat, you know."

He licked one paw, then sprang from my chest so abruptly that what little air I had in them shot from my lungs. As I sat up, I caught a glimpse of the golden braid uncoiling from around the railing, then whisking out of sight inside the tower.

Still more wizardry, I thought. Did that great shining mass actually possess a life of its own?

Melisande reached down and helped me to my feet.

"Don't be afraid," she said. "Nothing here will harm you."

If you say so, I thought.

Melisande took a step forward, toward the open pane of glass. Almost before I realized what I was doing, I stopped her, clutching tightly at her arm. Suddenly I was dizzy standing at the top of that tower, made of the bones of the earth and topped by the light of only-a-wizard-knew-how-many stars. The air blew cold against my skin, and it seemed to me that it was a very, very long way down to the ground. A very long way from anything I knew or understood.

"What happens if I cannot help?" I panted. "If I try and fail? What happens to your daughter then?"

What happens to me? Will you still love me? I thought.

"Nothing but what happens to us all," Melisande replied after a moment. "My daughter will grow old and die. During the years she has been imprisoned in this place, time has not moved in the same way for Rue as it has for you and me. Her days have been a waking dream, peaceful and quiet. At the turning of each year, she has aged a single day, no more. With our coming, time has resumed its normal course. Whether you leave or stay, whether you succeed or fail, from this day forward, Rue will move through time as the rest of us."

"Merciful heavens," I whispered, appalled at the ramifications of Melisande's words. Rue had been safe, in a way, while she'd been left alone. But our very coming had set in motion a sequence of events that could not be stopped. Now the sorceress's daughter would no longer be spared the passage of time. Instead, she would be free to count every single moment of her captivity. This would be the only freedom I would give her, if I failed to find the way to awaken her heart.

"What have we done?" I whispered.

And Melisande answered simply, "What we must."

I looked at her then, standing still as the cold wind at the top of the tower blew against us both. It came to me, in that moment, that Melisande was old. For more years than I had been alive she had carried the wizard's curse within her heart. She could have let it turn her hard and bitter, but she had not. Instead she had found room inside her heart for me. She had kept her hopes for her daughter alive.

How strong her heart must be, I thought. Could mine learn to be as strong?

That was the moment I thought I understood. I could let two days of pain and confusion wipe away all the love that had come before. I could make that the full measure of my heart. If I did, I would fail us all, but myself the most.

No, I thought. *I will not repay love with selfishness. I will not bring down such a curse upon myself.*

Yes, I was afraid, clear through to the marrow of my bones. But I could not afford to take the easy way out. I would not let my fear be stronger than my hope. I would take this test, of my own free will.

"We might as well go in, then," I said. And prayed that, when I discovered my heart's true strength, it would be strong enough.

It could have been no more than fifteen paces from the tower railing to those great and shimmering panes of glass, one of which stood open to allow us inside. But moving across that short distance seemed to take as many years as I had been alive.

Now that I was close upon them, I could see that the panes were curiously made, curved even as the tower itself was. Their surfaces were as shiny as mirrors. I could not see through them to the tower's inside. I could see only my reflection and Melisande's as we stood together. I had my favorite kerchief on, the one with the black-eyed Susans embroidered on it that Harry had given me long ago.

At the thought of Harry, I stopped dead. *So much for promising to stay out of trouble*, I thought.

"Rapunzel?" said Melisande.

"Coming," I said. I walked the last two paces, trying very hard not to think about Harry, and stepped inside.

It was beautiful. I swear to you that this was my very first thought, as every other fled in wonder from my mind.

The room at the tower's top was high-ceilinged, soaring upward on great wings of stone. Far from being the cold gray it had seemed at first, the stone now seemed to give off its own light, glowing warm and golden. In the room's center, protected by an elaborate wrought-iron railing much like the one outside, a great staircase curved down. Beyond that, I could see a loom strung with all the colors of the rainbow. Its shape contained the only straight lines I had yet seen in this place.

But it was the young woman standing beside the loom who drew and held my eyes.

She was about my age, just as Melisande had said she would be, though that was the wizardry at work, of course. Slim and straight and taller than I was, with skin so fair I could see the blue veins running underneath, see the throb of the pulse at her temple and throat. Without thinking, I counted the beats and so discovered that they precisely matched my own. Her eyes were a color I had seen only in the garden. Dark, like the faces of pansies.

Beautiful, I thought once more.

But frozen, like a plant that had bloomed too soon and been caught by a sudden frost. The sorceress's daughter still possessed her outward form. But inside, it seemed to me that everything was brittle, holding its breath, as if waiting to discover if the next thing to come along would be the frost that would kill it, or the thaw that would bring it back to life.

I will be that force of nature, I thought. By my actions, I would determine both Rue's future and my own.

She moved, then, almost as if she'd heard me, as if I had spoken my troublesome thought aloud. No more than a tilt of her head, a shift of her shoulders, but it was enough. Enough to show me that my eyes had deceived me in one thing: It wasn't the stone giving off the golden light. It wasn't the stone at all.

Flowing over the young woman's shoulders, running the length of her body to curve in great shining coils at her feet, was the braid that Melisande and I had used to scale the tower. It was this that caused the room to glow as if alive, burning with its own inner fire. I had a feeling it would shine, just like this, even in the dead of night.

Hair, I thought.

Hair such as I had imagined only in my dreams. Hair as bright and shining as the sun. As golden as the petals of the flowers I had been forced to leave behind in our back garden.

If I could have wept then, I would have done it. But beneath Rue's violet gaze, my eyes were as dry as the stone walls that suddenly seemed to close in all around. *No wonder her mother heard the sound of a door opening*, I thought. At that moment, I could almost hear it myself. I could see the way that Rue and I might fit together. Two halves of the same circle. The lock and the key.

Then her gaze shifted, and Rue looked at Melisande. As their eyes met, a strange ripple of movement seemed to pass through them both, and I saw the sorceress press a hand to her heart. But whether it was because she felt a sudden stab of pain or joy, I could not tell.

Rue's lips parted, and she drew in a breath. "Mama," she said, her voice sounding musical and rusty all at once. Like a fine instrument that has gone unused for many years but has not yet forgotten how to sound a tone.

"Mama?" she said once more, a question this time, her voice stronger and more urgent.

"Rue. My child," said Melisande.

I did weep then, as I watched the sorceress and her daughter slowly move together until each had stepped into the other's outstretched arms.

Eleven

It was the cat who decided things, in the end. A turn of events I don't think any of us, not even Melisande, could have foretold. Not that I made the final decision to stay and help lightly. It was merely that Mr. Jones enabled me to catch a glimpse of something I might not have been able to see on my own. And this turned out to be what tipped the scales and changed the balance, weighing it down on Rue's side.

Prior to that particular moment, however, in spite of all my noble intentions, it was pretty touch and go. It's one thing to think you understand what the right thing to do is. Actually doing it isn't always as straightforward, or as noble, as it sounds.

"Rapunzel, this is my daughter, Rue," Melisande said, once we had all shed tears for our own reasons and things had settled down. "Rue, this is Rapunzel, who is our hope."

She looked at me then with those violet eyes. In them I could read absolutely nothing at all. When Rue looked at her mother, her eyes seemed vivid and alive. But when she looked at me, they were flat and dull. I recognized the look; it seemed I was not the only one who was afraid and unwilling to show it.

"Why?" she asked simply.

Well, that's getting right to the point, I thought.

"Because I love her as I have loved no one else but you," Melisande answered, as honestly as always. "I hope this love may help her break the curse that binds you."

"She's supposed to find the way to free me?" Rue asked, and all of us could hear the disbelief in her voice. "But why can't you do it? I thought it would be you. You were the one who—"

I pulled in an audible breath and Rue broke off.

"I thought so too, for a time," Melisande answered after a moment. "But when I saw Rapunzel, I began to see another way, and so I made room for her inside my heart, took her in, and raised her as my own."

Rue's eyes flickered to me, and then away. They definitely held emotion now.

"All this time," she said. "She's been with you the whole time we've been kept apart?"

"Not all of it," Melisande answered, and I thought I could hear the effort she was making to keep her voice steady and calm. This meeting was hard on all of us. "Just the last sixteen years or so."

"I've been trapped in this tower, waiting," Rue continued, as if her mother hadn't spoken. "And you've been trying to replace me. You've been loving someone else."

"That's not altogether true," I said quietly. "Your mother loves me and I love her. That much is true enough. But she's never tried to replace you. She's never even let me call her mother. I think her heart is big enough to hold the both of us."

"What do you know about it?" Rue flashed out. "I never asked for your opinion, in case you didn't notice."

"Well, if I didn't," I came right back, "it's probably because I was distracted by the sight of you feeling sorry for yourself."

"I have a right to be unhappy," Rue began.

"Of course you do," I said. "But so do I. A week ago I had my very own bed, and apple trees to climb. My life wasn't perfect, but at least I had the illusion that it was mine. As of today, I've been dragged halfway across the country only to be informed that the reason your mother raised me in the first place was to help break the curse that keeps you in this tower.

"I learned about you yesterday, I'm meeting you for the first time today, and I have yet to decide whether or not I like you. What makes you think I'm any happier about all this than you are?"

"Well, don't expect me to ask you to stay," Rue said. "As far as I'm concerned, you can go whenever you want."

"Fine," I said. "Nice meeting you." I turned to her mother. "I'd like to go back down now."

"Rapunzel," said Melisande.

"No," I said. "I'm sorry, but no. 'Of my own free will,' you said. But she has to ask, some part of her has to want me to stay, or there's no point in this at all. I'm right and you know it."

"But I don't want you," Rue said. "I want—"

"I know, I know," I said. "You want a knight in shining armor."

"What's wrong with that?" Rue demanded.

"Not a thing," I responded. "But I'm not making any promises."

"You'll never get anything accomplished with an attitude like that."

"No, *we'll* never get anything accomplished unless you ask me to stay in the first place," I all but shouted.

We eyed each other for a moment, both of us breathing just a little too hard.

That was the moment the cat intervened. Bounding up the spiral staircase to pounce upon the ribbon at the end of Rue's hair. I hadn't thought about Mr. Jones since our arrival. But now here he was, a great fat copper penny wrestling with all that gold.

"Oh," Rue breathed. "A cat. Whose cat is it? Is it yours?"

At the tone of her daughter's voice, Melisande went very still. Together, we watched as Rue knelt and ran her fingers over Mr. Jones's fur. A moment later, his rich purr filled the room.

"Does it have a name?"

"Of course it has a name," I said. "It is a he and his name is Mr. Jones."

Rue was sitting on the floor now, sitting on her own hair, though I don't think she noticed. If you can let people climb up your hair, sitting on it yourself probably counts as nothing.

"That's a silly name for a cat," she said, at which he crawled up into her lap as if he'd known her all his life, turned around three times, then curled up with his tail tucked beneath him, just the way he always did in my lap.

I felt a pang in my heart. *So that's the way things are going to be*, I thought.

"He's named for the person who gave him to me," I explained. "A tinker, called Mr. Jones. He has ginger whiskers. It was meant to be a compliment to all concerned, and it seemed a good idea at the time."

"Can we keep him?" Rue suddenly inquired. She looked up. Not at her mother, but straight at me, and now I could see the way those violet eyes could shine. Almost as brightly and beautifully as all that golden hair. "If you were to stay, could he stay too?"

"I hope so," I said simply. "For I love him."

Her expression changed then, and Melisande became even more still than before, so still she could have been one of the stones of the tower.

"Would you, could I—"

Rue exhaled a frustrated breath and began again, though I noticed she no longer met my eyes, but kept hers fixed on Mr. Jones.

"If you stayed, would you be willing to share him with me? Could I learn to love him as well?"

I took one very deep breath of my own, held it for a count of six, then let it out.

"I would be willing to share him," I said. "But

whether or not you can learn to love him, only your heart can decide."

At this, Rue looked back up, her eyes wide. "You love him, but you would be willing to share," she said, as if she didn't quite trust that she'd heard me right the first time. "You wouldn't try to keep him all to yourself."

"Yes, I would share," I said. "Or at least I would try. That's the best thing to do with love, so I've always been told. If you can make room in your heart for the cat, I can make room in mine for the fact that you love him."

Her face changed then, her features slowly transforming themselves into an expression that I recognized: hope. Unexpected hope, at that, which is often the strongest kind.

"How would it work?" she asked, turning to her mother. "If I ask her to stay. How long?"

"Her name is Rapunzel," Melisande said. "You'll probably want to learn to say it. Together, the two of you must find the way to free you in the time it took to imprison you in the first place: two nights, the day that falls between, and the blink of an eye."

"Oh, for crying out loud!" I exclaimed. "Make it challenging, why don't you?"

"It isn't me . . . ," Melisande began.

"It's the wizard," I interrupted, "I know. You don't have to tell me. I'm beginning to think this world would have been a much better place if he'd simply learned to keep his mouth shut."

At this, Rue turned her head to look at me and did the very last thing I expected: She smiled. Before I quite knew what I was doing, I smiled back. Mr. Jones opened his mouth and gave a great, teeth-gnashing yawn. Rue's smile got a little bigger, and I felt my own hope suddenly kindle.

We can do this, I thought.

"Go ahead," I said. "It's not so difficult, once you put your mind to it. Just ask."

Rue gave a sigh, almost as if she'd hoped the fact that she already loved my cat meant I was going to let her off the hook.

"Will you stay with me, Rapunzel? Even though the outcome is uncertain?"

"Though the outcome is uncertain, I will stay with you, Rue," I said. "I will do my best to free us both."

And so the promise was made, and a bargain struck.

TWELVE

I cannot tell you what was said at the second parting between the sorceress and her daughter. It hardly seemed right for me to overhear it, so I went back out of that great golden room the same way I'd come, then walked around the tower's top until I could see the river and Mr. Jones, both far below me. I stood for a moment with my hands on the railing, as he looked up, and I looked down.

"You are going to stay, then," he said, his voice reaching me easily.

"I am," I said. "Though not for long, assuming all goes well. I'm to free the sorceress's daughter in the same time it took to make her a prisoner: two nights, the day that falls between, and the blink of an eye. How did you know? That I would stay, I mean."

"I didn't," the tinker answered. "I only thought you might."

"It's that heart thing again, isn't it?" I said, and, to my relief, we both smiled.

"Something like that," the tinker agreed. "Have you thought about what you'll tell Harry? He's going to want some sort of explanation, you know."

I felt the tower sway beneath my feet then, though my head knew it hadn't moved at all. Harry. I'd forgotten all about Harry. Again.

"No, I can see that you haven't," said Mr. Jones.

"I didn't mean . . . I never thought . . . ," I said.

"Take a deep breath," Mr. Jones said. "Stay calm. I'm sure you'll think of something when the time comes. You seem to have done all right so far."

"Where will you go? What will you do?" I asked. For, now that my brain was thinking beyond the tower, it seemed to me unlikely that the tinker and the sorceress would simply sit at its base and gaze upward for seventy-two hours, no matter how much Melisande might want to.

"I have traveled in this land a little," Mr. Jones said. "There is a town about a day's journey through the forest, the seat of the king who rules these parts. That's as good a place to go as any."

"What of Melisande?"

"You'd better ask her that yourself," the tinker said. At this, I turned to discover the sorceress standing by my side.

"Ask me what?" said Melisande.

"I was wondering whether or not you'd go with him," I said. "He's going to the closest town. I think I'd feel better knowing the two of you were together."

"Are you asking me to do this?" Melisande said, and I thought I could see the barest hint of a twinkle at the back of her eyes.

One good question deserves another, I thought.

"Yes, I am asking you to do this," I said. "For my sake, will you please stay with Mr. Jones?"

"Gladly," Melisande replied. "For your sake, as well as my own."

With that, before I quite realized what she intended, she reached out and enfolded me in her arms. A thousand memories seemed to rush through me, as if summoned of their own accord.

The sorceress and I sitting before the fire on a winter's night as she patiently taught my fumbling fingers to knit. Standing in the kitchen on a hot summer's day, laughing as we realized that every single one of our mutual twenty fingers was stained the exact same color from picking blueberries the whole morning long. I remembered lying in my bed at night when I was supposed to be asleep, gazing instead at where Melisande sat brushing out her hair. Wondering if I would ever have hair of my own, knowing she would love me just the same even if I never did.

She loves me, I thought. Against all odds, and in the face of her own pain, she had made room for me inside her heart. Now the time had come for me to return the favor for her daughter, if I could.

"Thank you," she whispered, and she stepped back and let me go.

"Don't thank me yet," I answered. "I haven't done very much."

She raised her eyebrows at this. "You think not?"

"I'll do what I can," I said.

"That's all that can be asked of anyone," she replied.

With that, almost as if she was moving quickly before either of us could change our minds, the sorceress spoke the password once more.

"One so fair, let down your hair. Let me go from here to there."

No sooner had she spoken than the pane of glass behind us flew open and Rue's great golden braid came flying out. Once, twice it wrapped itself around the railing, just as it had before, them plummeted down to land beside the tinker with a *plunk*. Melisande gave me a final kiss, then, without another word, climbed down. As soon as her feet touched the greensward, the braid ascended, *whoosh*ing out of sight, and the pane of glass closed silently behind it.

"We'll see you in a couple of days," Mr. Jones called up. "When Harry finally gets here, tell him we've gone on to the town. He can follow if he wants to. He can't get lost. All he has to do is keep to the main road."

"I'll do that," I said. "Assuming he speaks to me at all."

"Oh, he'll speak to you," the tinker answered. "I have a feeling you can count on that."

Then he helped Melisande into the wagon and clucked once to the horse. I stood at the railing, waving until they were out of sight and then some. Finally I turned around. The great bank of windows at the tower's top showed me nothing but my own reflection, with the sky at my back.

Was Rue on the other side of the closest one? I wondered. Had she watched me say farewell to her mother?

Stop it, Rapunzel, I chastised myself. *If you start off thinking of this as a competition, the whole exercise will be nothing but a waste of time.*

Time, the one thing I could not afford to waste. Holding that fact firmly in my mind, I crossed the stone balcony, whose width was fifteen paces but felt like a hundred, and went back inside.

Rue had remained sitting right where I'd left her, at the top of the steps with Mr. Jones in her lap. She was teasing the cat with the end of that long, long braid.

"Does it hurt?" I asked suddenly. "When people go up and down?"

"No," she answered, with a quick shake of her head. "I don't feel it at all. I don't think I feel much of anything, to tell you the truth."

I was silent for a moment, taking this in. "Maybe it's just a side effect of all this wizardry," I suggested. "Something that will wear off."

"I'm not so sure I want it to," Rue answered, with an honesty that would have made her mother proud. "It's safer not to feel anything, don't you think? Besides, I'm used to it by now."

I thought of the life to which I'd been accustomed,

just one short week ago. Having it all yanked away so abruptly had definitely been painful. In spite of the fact that I felt I could almost see time racing by me, I decided to go slowly now.

"It may have to wear off, sooner or later," I suggested gently. "The curse does say something about awakening your heart."

"Oh, so now you're the expert?" she asked, her tone ever so slightly sarcastic. "What makes you think you know anything about it? You're not the one who's been stuck up here for time out of mind."

Okay, I thought. *So much for going slow.* If this was the way things were going to be, might as well throw myself off the tower right this second and be done with it. Better yet, I'd throw her off.

"For someone who claims she doesn't feel anything, you're awfully quick to pick a fight," I remarked.

"Am not."

"Are too."

Rue gave a sudden snort and looked up then, her violet eyes laughing. "I suppose you think you're pretty smart."

"No, I don't," I said. "If I was smart, we'd both be out of here by now."

I could have kicked myself as I saw the laughter drain away as if I'd poked a hole in a bucket full of water.

"I wouldn't worry about it very much if I were you," she said. "We both know I'm never getting out of here anyhow."

"We do not know that," I answered, stung. "Why is there nothing to sit on in this stupid place?"

At this, the smile returned, though it wasn't a very cheerful one. "There's a stool at the loom," she said. "You could try that."

I fetched it and placed it where I could sit facing her.

"We are going to do this," I said firmly. "We're going to figure out the way to get you out. Putting you here was wrong and cruel. It should never have happened in the first place."

I could feel her resistance start to waver, even as I watched her shore it up. I was familiar with the sensation.

"If you say so," she replied.

"There you are, doing it again," I cried. I got to my feet, in spite of the fact that I'd just finished sitting down. "Acting as if you're the only one who's ever had to face a problem. I've got news for you: You're not. What's the matter? Are you so afraid you'll fail that you'd prefer not to try at all?"

Oh, right, Rapunzel, I thought, even as I heard myself speak. *As if the thought hadn't crossed your mind.*

"Of course not," Rue answered, her cheeks coloring. "It's just . . ." She swallowed then, a convulsive motion of her throat, and I realized how close she was to tears. "I've been in this tower for as long as I can remember. I'm afraid to ask *how* long. What if I can't remember how to live like other people? What if I'm broken and can't be fixed? What if I . . . you know."

"I don't," I said, which was the absolute truth.

"Love," she said loudly, causing Mr. Jones to give a startled and indignant meow. "What if I can't fall in love?"

"Of course you can fall in love," I said.

"You don't know that," she countered.

"Okay," I said, as I sank slowly back down upon the stool. "All right. Officially, maybe I don't. But you said you wanted to learn to love Mr. Jones. I'd say that's a good sign."

"It doesn't matter," Rue said quickly. "Nobody's ever going to want me anyhow."

"What are you talking about?" I asked.

"Look at me," she cried out. "Look. *Look.* Use your eyes!"

"Let me tell you what I see," I said. "You have skin as fine as any angel cake I ever baked. Your eyes are a color poets dream of writing about, and your hair is as golden and bountiful as a dragon's hoard. You may see these things as posing a problem, but believe me, you'll be the only one who does."

"You think *this* is beautiful?" Rue said. She shot to her own feet now, seizing her long, golden braid with both hands and shaking it as if it were a snake that she would like to choke the life right out of. Mr. Jones leaped from her lap in alarm and disappeared out of sight down the great curved staircase.

"You try living with it for a while. I trip over it

when I walk. Get tangled up in it when I sleep. I can't cut it—the wizard took care of that. My own mother has to climb my hair just to come and visit. If this doesn't make me a freak, I don't know what does."

"At least you have some," I said.

"Have what?"

"Hair," I replied.

At this, all the fight seemed to drain right out of her. She rubbed a hand across her brow.

"I don't understand a word you're saying," she said.

I reached up for my kerchief, pulled it off.

"Oh," Rue said, and her mouth made the exact same shape in surprise. Slowly she sank back down to the floor. "Oh, my."

"That's one way of putting it," I said. In that moment, I realized how tired I was. "How about this," I proposed. "Let's both avoid the word 'freak,' shall we?'"

"Good. That sounds good," Rue nodded. She fell silent for a moment as we gazed at one another. "I suppose I can see now why Mama thought this might work," she finally remarked. "There is a certain symmetry involved. Does it hurt?" she asked, her question the exact same as my own just minutes ago.

"No," I said. "Not unless I get clumsy and run it into something hard and unyielding." *Sort of like you*, I thought. I put the kerchief back on.

"This really might work," Rue said cautiously

after another moment. "Given the actual circumstances, I mean."

"I suppose," I said. "It might."

"Not that it means we always have to get along."

"Thanks goodness for that," I said.

She gave a snort. "Naturally you would agree with that."

"Perhaps I haven't any sense," I said. "Maybe it goes along with not having any hair."

"Oh, I know you haven't any sense," Rue replied. "If you had, you'd have climbed down all this unnecessary hair at the first available opportunity."

"I couldn't do that," I said. "I made a promise."

"To my mother, you mean."

"No," I said. "To myself."

We were both silent once more, while this thought slowly circled inside the tower, then came back to rest between us.

"Can you really make an angel cake?" Rue asked.

I nodded. "As tall as the oven door. I'll bake one for you on your wedding day. How would that be?"

She smiled then, a neither-here-nor-there sort of smile. Not quite joyful, but not sad, either. A smile that left the future open.

"I think that I would like that. Thank you, Rapunzel."

Before either of us could say another word, a new voice floated up the length of the tower.

"Parsley," it shouted. "What in heaven's name have you done?"

THIRTEEN

"Oh, dear," I said, as I shot to my feet. "I was afraid of this."

"Who on earth is that?" Rue asked as she, too, stood up. "And why is he calling you Parsley?"

"Because he's a wretched tinker's boy with no manners whatsoever," I said. "His name is Harry." *And the last time I saw him, he kissed me in my own front yard.*

"I know you're in there, Parsley," Harry's voice shouted once more. "I met the sorceress and Mr. Jones along the road. If you're not out where I can see you by the time I count to ten, I'm coming up to get you myself."

"He can't do that," Rue said.

"I know that and you know that," I said. "Even Harry may know. It's not going to make a single bit of difference. Harry is the reason somebody somewhere invented the word 'stubborn.'"

"One," his voice floated up from the bottom of the tower.

"I'm going to have to go out there," I said. "He'll only do something foolish and hurt himself."

"I'm not stopping you, am I?" Rue asked.

"Two. Threefourfive," Harry's voice said.

"Gee," I said. "Thanks for your support. It means the world to me. All right, Harry," I called back, lifting my voice so it would carry. "You've proven you can count. I'm coming."

With that, I simply moved to the pane of glass that seemed closest to the sound of his voice and pushed it open. Fifteen steps took me to the edge of the balcony. They only felt like about fifty this time around. When I got to the edge, I could see him standing far below. Our horse cropped the grass at his side. I was so relieved to see that he was safe, I almost forgot to be annoyed.

"So there you are, Parsley," he said. "It's about time."

"That's a fine thing for you to say," I came right back. "You're the one who's late, tinker's boy."

"I thought you were going to stay out of trouble," he said.

"I'm not in trouble. I'm in a tower," I replied.

"Oh, ha-ha," he said. "Very funny. You promised, or don't you recall?"

"Of course I do," I said. *I remember everything about the day we said good-bye.* "I'm not in trouble, Harry. Honestly, I'm not. I'm doing something for Melisande."

"Staying with her daughter," he nodded. "I know. I told you. I met them on the road. That's why I was late. I had to make a detour around a band of soldiers. Some unrest is brewing in this land. I'm not so sure it's any safer than the one we left behind."

"You'd better catch up with them, then," I said. "It might not be safe for you to be on your own."

Harry shook his head, and even from high above I recognized the stubborn set of his jaw.

"Not until I know that you're all right," he said.

"Harry," I said, doing my best to sound patient even when I didn't particularly feel that way. "I'm fine. This tower is protected by a wizard's magic. No one can get up here unless they know how to ask properly."

"The sorceress said there was a password," he admitted. He kicked irritably at the perfect swath of grass that surrounded the tower. "She wouldn't tell me what it was."

"That's as it should be," I said. "Now go away and come back with Mr. Jones and Melisande."

"Stop doing that," he suddenly said, and he used the foot that had been kicking grass to get in a good old-fashioned stomp. "Stop treating me as if you were all grown up and important and I'm no more than an irritating child. I haven't seen you for six days. I worried about you, dammit."

"I worried about you, too," I said.

"You might have waited for me, you know."

"I'm sorry, Harry," I said. "I didn't think I could."

He gave the grass one last stab with his toe.

"So, what's she like?"

"Who?" I said.

"Don't be stupid, Parsley," Harry said. "The sorceress's daughter, of course."

"As beautiful as an angel," I said.

"Fine. Don't tell me."

"I'm telling you the truth," I protested. And then a thought occurred to me. "Stay here. I'll be right back."

"Rapunzel, wait," Harry called. But by then, I'd already turned and marched back inside the tower. Rue was standing beside the window I'd left open, staring out as if she could see Harry far below.

"I need you to come outside," I said.

Rue backed up a step, her eyes growing wide. "What are you talking about?" she asked, as her already pale cheeks turned the even paler color of chalk. "I can't go outside. You know that."

"Not *outside* outside," I said. "Just out onto the balcony. I want Harry to see you, so he knows I'm all right."

Rue shook her head, the light dancing across her hair the same way it did upon water.

"I can't go out," she said again.

"Can't, or won't?" I asked. I put my hands on my hips as a sudden suspicion occurred. "I'll bet you've never even tried."

She opened her mouth, seemed to think better of whatever she'd been about to say, and closed it with a snap.

"You're right," she admitted after a moment. "I've never even tried. There were times when I thought I wanted to. But then I thought, I feared, that if I tried and failed, it must surely break my heart."

Because her words made perfect sense, I moved to her and put a hand on her arm. She flinched, ever so slightly, though I don't think she minded the gesture. It was that, compared with the chill of her skin, mine felt so warm. My first impression had been right, I thought. The sorceress's daughter was like a plant held in thrall by a sudden frost. I would have to find the way to thaw her out. In this moment, I thought I saw how to make at least a start.

"What if you tried and succeeded?" I asked. "What might that do to your heart?"

"I haven't the faintest idea," she said. "But . . ." She took a breath and looked me straight in the eye. "If you ask me to go, I'll do my best."

I gave a quick laugh almost before I knew what I had done.

"That does seem only fair," I said. "Not to mention very sneaky of you. But very well: Will you please accompany me out onto the balcony, Rue?"

"Are you coming with me?" she asked.

"Absolutely," I answered.

"In that case, I think I would like to try."

"No changing your mind at the very last minute," I said. "If you do, I'm just going to drag you out anyhow. By all that hair, most likely."

"Thanks for your support. It means the world to me," she said, parroting my own words. But I could see the fear, rising like a tide in those lovely violet eyes.

"It's just a few steps, Rue," I said, as I linked my arm through hers. "You can do this."

"Okay," she said. "If you say so."

It was all of about six steps from where we stood to the pane of glass that let out onto the balcony. I solemnly swear they were the longest steps I'd ever taken in my life. Longer even than the time it had taken me to get from the balcony to the tower. How long the distance felt to Rue, I cannot tell.

"Just one more step," I finally said. And then, at last, we were standing outside. Rue raised a hand to shield her eyes.

"It's so bright," she said. "Okay, I did it. I think I'd like to go back in now."

"You have *not* done it," I said firmly, as I kept ahold of her arm. "We have to go all the way to the railing, so Harry can see you."

"Rapunzel," his voice floated up at precisely that moment. "What's happening up there? What's going on?"

"Just another minute, Harry," I called. "There's someone I'd like you to meet." I turned back to Rue. "It's only fifteen paces more. We can even count them out, if you think that will help."

"There's no need to treat me like a child," Rue snapped.

"Fine," I answered. "Then stop acting like one."

There's a reason that daring people to accept a challenge almost always works. Put fear and pride head to head, and pride will win almost every single time. At my words Rue lifted her chin, even as her eyes continued to squint against the outdoor sunlight, and yanked her arm from mine.

"I'm not a child," she said. "I'm not." Then, gathering up as much of that fat golden braid as her arms would carry, she marched the fifteen paces to the railing and looked down.

"You must be Harry," she said. "My name is Rue, and I'm very pleased to meet you." She let her hair drop down onto the balcony with a *thunk*.

There was a pause. In it I could hear the wind moving through the trees of the forest. The water of the river moving over stones. The croak of frogs at the water's edge. Birdsong.

Then Harry said, "Thank you. That's right. Harry. Yes. Harry. Thank you very much."

At that, I made it to the railing in record time. Fifteen paces that actually felt like less. Because, as Harry had spoken, I'd felt my heart give a sudden clutch. I gripped the railing, staring downward at him. He had lifted a hand as if he were dazzled, as if he were staring straight into the sun, when, in fact, it was behind him. Then he dropped it, and I could see the expression on his face.

Merciful heavens, I thought. *What have I done?*

It was Rue, of course. Even inside, she'd seemed to give off her own light. But in the true light of day, she was all but blinding. Her hair caught the sunlight and sent it back so that it gleamed like an enormous heap of newly minted coins. Even her dress, which I had thought as plain and simple as my own, I suddenly discovered to be shot through with golden thread, so that it glinted with every breath she took. Her face, so fearful and uncertain just moments before, was now filled with an intrigued delight.

I could almost hear the crack of the ice that had contained her, could almost see it be swept away, even as I saw Rue herself begin to come to life.

Beautiful, I thought, just as I had when I had seen her for the very first time. The most beautiful thing I'd seen in my entire life. And all of that beauty, all that awakening light, was streaming straight down at the young man I loved.

I turned away then and sank slowly down to the stone of the balcony, my back pressed against the railing. For I was afraid that, if I stood up straight for one moment longer, I would fall. That's what my heart was doing, a long slow tumble through space on its way to I wasn't quite sure what destination. Uncertain outcome.

When had it happened? I wondered. When had my heart decided that what it felt for the tinker's boy was love?

Had it been the day he'd given me the kerchief? The kiss, so unexpected and so sweet, that last day in the yard? Could it even have been that very first night we'd met, when I had seen the way his fingers had reached up to gently stroke the nose of the horse he'd convinced himself he wanted to steal but knew in his own heart of hearts that he would not?

Or maybe, I thought, as my heart finally caught up with my body and seemed to come to rest, though not particularly comfortably, it was only now. Now, when I realized that it all might be for nothing. The moment I saw what it would mean if he didn't love me back, when I had seen him blinded by Rue's shining, golden light. This was the moment I knew that what I felt for the tinker's boy was love.

"Heavens, Rapunzel," her voice suddenly said, from what sounded like a very long way above my head. "Are you all right?"

"Fine," I said. "I just got a little dizzy, that's all. It's a long way down." *A long way to fall.*

"But it's so beautiful out here," she said. "You were right, to urge me to come."

"I'm glad, Rue," I said. "Honestly, I am."

She bent over me then, a frown snaking down between her eyebrows. I bit down on my tongue to hold back the bubble of hysterical laughter that threatened to explode right out of my chest. *Even her eyebrows are golden*, I thought.

"You're sure you're all right?" she said once more.

"No. Yes. Of course I am," I said.

"What is it?" I heard Harry's voice call. "What's going on?"

"Something seems to be the matter with Rapunzel," Rue called back.

"Rapunzel?" Harry echoed. And at that, so great a dizziness swept over me that I actually put my head down between my knees. He sounded as if he didn't even know who I was.

"Yes, Rapunzel," I said, as I forced myself to my feet. The world seemed to sway as I looked down. "You remember me, don't you?"

"What are you talking about? Of course I remember you," Harry said. He put his hands on his hips. "I'm not so sure I think you should stay up there. I think that tower may be affecting your mind."

Not my mind, I thought. *It's not my mind at all.*

"She does act strangely sometimes, doesn't she?" Rue suddenly asked, her voice as delighted as I'd ever heard it.

"You have no idea," Harry replied.

"Okay, that's it," I said. "Rue, I think it's time to go back in now."

"But I just came out," she protested. "I like it out here. You were right."

"You could get a sunburn," I said. "It hurts a lot. I should know. I really think you should come back in right this minute." I took her by the arm and began to tug her away from the railing, back toward the tower's inside.

"Stop it!" she snapped. "You're hurting my arm." She tugged against my grip. "Good-bye, Harry," she called. "I hope you'll come back and visit us tomorrow. Maybe Rapunzel"—she gave her arm a hard enough jerk to free it—"will have recovered her senses by then. Though personally," she whispered for my ears alone, "I doubt it."

"Of course I'll come back," Harry said. "In fact, I'm thinking it might be a good idea if I stuck around. There are still those armed men to consider."

"What are you talking about?" I asked.

"I told you," Harry said. "It's the reason I was late in the first place. I spotted a band of armed men I decided it would be better to avoid. They could still be roaming around."

"So you're going to sit around here and wait for them to show up?" I inquired. "What good will that do? They can't come up here any more than we can come down."

"Well, I think it would be lovely if Harry stayed," Rue put in. "It will give me somebody to talk to."

"What's the matter?" I asked. "Don't I count?"

"Not at the moment, you don't," Rue replied.

"I'll see you tomorrow, then," Harry said. "I hope you feel better, Parsley."

"My name," I said through clenched teeth, "is Rapunzel."

Then I turned and marched back inside the tower.

FOURTEEN

"I don't understand what's the matter with you," Rue said, as she came in right behind me. "I did what you asked. I met your friend. He seems nice."

"He certainly seemed to like you," I answered shortly.

"What's that supposed to mean?" she said. "I thought . . . ," she stopped, and, to my horror, I watched as her eyes filled with tears. "Don't you *want* him to like me?"

"Of course I do," I said. I'd thought I'd already experienced the most miserable day of my life, followed shortly by the most painful and confusing. Now I knew that I'd been wrong. Today was much worse than either one of those, for it combined all those elements into one.

I can't blame Rue, I thought. That would be taking the coward's way out. How could I blame her for failing to notice what I hadn't noticed myself until now? The fact that the only way I realized I was in love with Harry was by watching him fall for her like a ton of bricks could hardly be considered Rue's fault.

"Don't pay any attention to me. I'm sorry."

Rue stared at me for one long moment. "I've come

to the conclusion that you are impossible," she declared.

"I know that," I said. "I know it."

"The most impossible brat it's ever been my misfortune to know. Stop doing that, by the way. And stop interrupting."

"Stop doing what?" I asked.

"Agreeing with me at exactly the moment you're not supposed to."

I could feel my lips start to twitch into a smile, even as my heart wanted to weep. She was waking up by leaps and bounds now.

"I solemnly swear never to agree with you again," I said. "Not only that, I apologize."

"Impossible. Definitely," Rue said. We stood, face to face, and regarded each other for a while. "Something just happened, didn't it?" she said. "Something important. I'm just not sure I know what it was."

"You went outside," I said. "You proved you don't have to be a prisoner anymore. Now all we have to do is to figure out how to find that stupid door."

"And how to open it. Don't forget that part."

"I'm not likely to," I responded.

Find the door. Open it so Rue could be free. Free to walk out of the tower and straight into Harry's waiting arms.

That night I could not sleep. Not surprising, I suppose. In the first place, there was the undeniable fact that I felt I ought to be doing something other than sleeping. I only had tonight, tomorrow, and the night that followed, after all. But, though I racked my brains, I couldn't think of a single, solitary act I should, or could, be performing.

I'd walked the tower from the top to the bottom, climbing up and down that great curving stair until my legs ached, and seen no sign of any door. Rue had sat at her loom, passing the shuttle back and forth, and hadn't said a word. Not long after, the sun had gone down in a great blaze of red, and I had given up entirely. After a while, Rue had gathered Mr. Jones up in her arms and gone to sleep. But my eyes stayed wide open.

How can I help her? I thought. How could I find the way to free Rue's heart, when I could no longer find my own?

For it seemed to me that my heart was lost. It roamed through some vast, uncharted wilderness, like the forest I could see when I looked out from the tower's top. It was dark where my heart roamed. The territory was so unfamiliar that, merely by setting foot within it, my heart had lost its way. It might wander in this dark place forever and never be found.

What if it's never even missed? I thought. At this my fear grew so great that my body could no longer remain still. I got up, and, on feet as silent as I could make them, I moved to the closest pane of glass, pushed it open, and stepped outside. The bright, clear day had been followed by an all but moonless night. The sky above me was a great and single sweep of dark. In it the stars sparkled like water drops. I found the closest one. Or maybe it was simply the biggest, pulsing now blue, now white.

"I don't even know what to wish for," I said, altogether failing to notice that I had spoken aloud. I often did this, particularly when I was troubled and trying to sort things out.

"I don't seem to know much of anything at all. How can I find the key to awaken someone else's heart, when I can't even keep track of my own?"

"Take mine."

I was glad I was nowhere near the railing, because the sound of a second voice so startled me that, if I'd been at the tower's edge, chances were good I'd have tumbled right off it in surprise.

"That isn't funny, Harry," I said.

"I wasn't joking," the voice replied. "I'm not Harry, either."

"What do you mean you're not Harry?" I said, though now that I knew to listen I had to acknowledge that the voice didn't sound quite right. "Who are you?"

"My name is Alexander," my unknown visitor replied. "Though most people simply say, 'Your Highness.'"

"Why would they do that?" I asked.

"Because I'm a prince," Alexander answered simply. "And you are?"

"Rapunzel."

"Pleased to make your acquaintance, Rapunzel," the voice claiming to be a prince named Alexander replied. "I don't suppose I could convince you to come out where I could get a better look at you?"

"It's too dark," I said at once. I was curious, I had to admit. Maybe I'd just had one too many surprises for one day, but I decided to stay right where I was. "There's no moon. It wouldn't make a difference anyhow."

"I suppose you're right," he said on what sounded suspiciously like a sigh. "Any chance I could convince you anyhow? I could say something princely and poetic. Something along the lines of love lending my eyes extra sight."

"You could," I acknowledged, as amusement began to take the place of shock. "But I wouldn't believe you, so you might as well save your breath. Are all princes this handy with words?"

"I think so," Alexander said. "All the ones I know are. It sort of goes along with the territory, I think. You know—diplomacy."

"So statescraft is only lies dressed up?"

"Of course not," he replied at once. "Though princes are taught early how to woo. It's how wars are averted, more often than not. Is your father worried about his neighbor? Fearful that he covets territory not his own? The solution is simple. Have your son marry the neighbor's daughter, never mind the fact that he hasn't set eyes upon her since she was six years old. Not that she's to know this is the cause, of course. Your number one duty, before anything else, is to convince her that your sudden devotion is nothing less than true love."

So that's the way it is, I thought. Now that my ears were learning how to listen, I could detect the strain of bitterness running through Prince Alexander's voice.

"I'm not a princess. You needn't practice your fine words on me."

"How can you not be a princess? You're in a tower."

"Good point," I said, beginning to be charmed in spite of myself. "Though it is an obvious one that changes nothing. I am still just plain Rapunzel." An idea was beginning to form in the back of my mind. So far it was just an outline. "Do princes see only what is right in front of them?" I asked.

"Some do, some don't," Alexander answered solemnly. "The best ones, the ones who grow up to be wise kings, know how to see what is there as well as what is not. That's what my father always says, anyhow."

"And will you master this skill, do you think?" I asked.

"I hope so," Alexander said. "For I am my father's only son."

"Oh, so you are on a quest, then," I said. "To help you gain wisdom and enlightenment."

"Not exactly," the prince answered with a snort. "I wasn't joking about the king of the neighboring kingdom. He really is thinking of invading, and his army is much larger than ours. My father and his council are seriously considering marrying me to the king's daughter as a means of negotiating a way out. I've tried to reconcile myself, but . . ."

His voice trailed off.

"I'm sorry," I said, and meant it. At least when it came to helping Rue, I'd had a genuine choice. It sounded very much like Prince Alexander had none.

"You're sure you're not a princess?" he asked, his tone wistful. "It would solve so much."

"Quite sure," I said. "Though I am held in this place by enchantment. Might that help?"

"Absolutely," Alexander said at once, his voice picking up. "Damsels in enchanted distress trump neighboring princesses every single time. Nothing could be better than you being enchanted, in fact, for the princess's father is terrified by magic of any kind. I shall rescue you. We'll get married and live happily ever after. Meanwhile the king and his soldiers slink home in disgrace. How does that sound?"

"Like a fine plan," I said. "Always assuming it can be accomplished."

"But that's where you come in," Alexander pronounced. "If you'll just give me even one clue about the best way to free you, it would be a great help. Enchanted maidens often do this, you know."

"Where I come from, we call that cheating," I said.

"No," he countered swiftly. "Not if it's done in the

cause of true love. If it's in the cause of true love, then we're in this together, striving against impossible odds."

"The only impossible thing around here is you," I said, though I did suddenly remember the way Rue had called me impossible only several hours before. At once, the idea that had been forming and re-forming in the back of my mind took a definite shape.

Rue, I thought. Rue, who feared she could never fall in love yet dreamed of being set free by a knight in shining armor. Not quite a description of Alexander, it was true, but pretty close.

"Why are you here?" I asked. "Why aren't you stargazing from the battlements of home? Tell me the truth. You have to, if you're going to attempt to free me in the cause of true love."

"The truth is that I ran away," he said, after a moment's pause. "And after that, I got lost. I encountered a band of our neighbor's soldiers in the woods. I think they were a scouting party. By the time I'd successfully avoided them, I realized I didn't have the faintest idea where I was. Then I saw the tower, and then I heard your voice."

"You could be in danger if you stay here, then," I said, suddenly alarmed.

"They were going in the opposite direction," Alexander said. "Please don't tell me I'd be better off at home. I might be safer, for a little while anyway, but not better off. The only way I'll go is if you come with me."

"I've already told you," I said. "This tower is enchanted. I can't just come down."

"Then I'll stay until I find the way to free you," Alexander said stubbornly. "A real prince never abandons his true love."

"I am not your true love," I said. "You just met me not five minutes ago."

"Haven't you ever heard of love at first sight?"

"Love at first sight, yes," I said. "Not love at first sound. You've never even seen me. You've only heard my voice."

He gave a quick, unexpected laugh, and, just as unexpectedly, I felt my heart leap at the sound. *Oh, he is perfect,* I thought.

"I think you're splitting hairs, Rapunzel," he said.

Not I, I thought. *Not I.* But though I could not see him, I thought I could see my way now. So much would depend upon Rue, which was only fair, as it was her heart I was trying to free anyhow.

"What makes you think I'd be any easier to live with than the neighbor king's daughter?" I inquired.

"Just one important thing," Alexander answered. "I can choose you for myself."

Perfect, indeed, I thought. Now all I had to do was find the way to bring Rue and this prince together.

"Do you really want to help me?" I asked.

"I do," he said at once.

"Then come back again, tomorrow night. Promise me you'll stay hidden during the day, so the soldiers won't find you."

"I promise," he vowed.

"I mean it, Alexander," I said. "If you show up in broad daylight, I won't come out at all, even if you call my name until you're hoarse. I'll refuse to speak to you ever again. You'll have to go home and marry the princess next door after all."

"I promise, Rapunzel," Prince Alexander said again. "If you will promise something as well."

"What?" I asked.

"Promise that, sometimes, you will call me Alex."

"You want me to call you Alex?" I asked. "That's all?"

Even from the top of the tower, I thought I heard him sigh. As if many things he'd held inside for far too long had finally been let go.

"Just once more?"

"Alex," I said.

"Thank you, Rapunzel."

"You're welcome. I'll see you tomorrow night." No more than a figure of speech, of course. "And remember your promise."

"I will," Alexander said. "Good night, my Rapunzel."

I opened my mouth to say I wasn't his Rapunzel at all, then closed it before I made a sound.

"Good night, Alex," I said instead.

"So!" he said. "Three times, and the third time works the charm."

I thought I heard him move off then, for there came a rustle from far below. Then, without warning,

I heard a sharp cry. I flew to the tower railing, my heart in my throat.

"It's never going to work, you know," a voice I knew quite well said.

"Harry," I hissed. "What have you done?"

FIFTEEN

"I didn't do a thing," Harry said at once. "I didn't need to. Your brave and handsome prince put his foot straight down a gopher hole, pitched forward into the trunk of the nearest tree, and knocked himself out. It's a miracle the soldiers didn't catch him earlier."

"You have to help him," I said. "Is he all right?"

"He'll be fine, Parsley," Harry said, and I shivered, for his voice seemed cold. "His head will probably be sore for a day or so. I'd thought better of you, I must admit."

"What are you talking about?" I demanded crossly. "And keep your voice down. I don't want to wake up Rue."

"Now why could that be, I wonder?" Harry inquired. "It couldn't have anything to do with the fact that you're planning to sneak off and leave her with nothing, I suppose?"

"Of course I'm not planning to do that," I said. "What are you talking about?"

"*Come back tomorrow night, Alex,*" Harry said, in a not particularly flattering imitation of my voice. "*Stay hidden during the day, so I'll know that you'll be safe.*"

"You think I'd do that," I said, a statement, not a question. "You think I'd turn my back on Melisande and her daughter while the promises I made them both are still warm in my mouth. Are you sure you're not judging me by yourself, Harry? You were the one who once planned to steal a horse belonging to a man who'd saved you from death itself, as I recall."

"Don't think you can make yourself look better by throwing my past in my face," Harry said. "I heard what I heard."

"So you did," I said. "And now you can hear this as well: Good night."

I turned to go.

"Don't walk away. Don't you dare walk away from me, Rapunzel," Harry cried. "You owe me an explanation."

"I don't owe you a thing," I said, and wondered that I could speak at all for the way the words scalded my throat. This was what he thought of me, then. That I had so little spine, so little honor, that I would leave Rue to an unhappy fate and break my own word in less than a night.

"My debt is to the sorceress and her daughter. I mean to pay it in whatever way I can. Don't think that you can judge me, tinker's boy."

"Why must you always do that?" he demanded.

"Do what?"

"Call me by the one name you know I dislike the very most."

"I suppose that would be why," I said. "Just as that's why you call me Parsley."

"Your name is Parsley," he said.

"My name *means* parsley," I replied. "It's not the same thing at all. Go to bed, Harry. It's been a long day. But first, make sure Alexander is all right."

"He's really that important to you," Harry said.

"Yes," I replied. "He's really that important."

Not just to me, but to all of us, I thought.

I know what some of you are thinking: Why didn't I just come right out and tell him? Why didn't I explain what I had in mind? Here is the only answer I can give you: If you have to ask, you've never been in love. More than that, you've never had your feelings hurt by the one you want to trust and cherish you most of all.

So I did not explain why Prince Alexander was so important to me. I would let that be a lesson the tinker's boy learned for himself.

In time. If all went well.

"There's a woodcutter's cottage, not far within the trees," Harry said. "It's old, but still well made and snug. I suppose there could be room for more than one. But don't expect me to wait on him or do his bidding. I wouldn't get your hopes up too high. He'll probably give up and wander off."

"Thank you, Harry," I said.

"I don't want your thanks," he answered shortly. "I'm not doing it for you. I'm doing it for Mr. Jones, and for Melisande. You're not the only one who knows how to discharge a debt."

"Thank you anyway," I said.

But my words were met with silence. Though I stayed on the balcony for many moments, listening with all my might, I heard only the sound of my own heart, and, high above my head, the wind, whispering secrets to the cold, unheeding stars.

"No!" Rue said. "Absolutely not!"

It was early evening on the second day. I had put off telling Rue what had happened for as long as I felt I could, a choice that had given me new sympathy for Melisande. There's something about knowing you have to tell someone something you know equally well they won't want to hear that definitely encourages you to hold your tongue.

I had to tell Rue sooner or later, though. The sun was about to go down.

"But it's the perfect solution. Don't you see?" I asked. "He already fancies himself half in love."

"With *you*," Rue said. "Half in love with *you*. I'm not a charity case, thank you very much. Besides, what's he going to do, call me Rapunzel?"

"What does it matter what he calls you?" I asked. "What's important is that he thinks it's love."

"But it would be a lie," Rue said. "A lie from the very beginning. How can a lie grow into true love?"

It was a good question, I had to admit, and one I had spent most of the day grappling with myself. I wasn't stupid. I could see the potential flaws in the plan I'd dreamed up so suddenly the night before, but I still thought it was worth a try.

Handsome princes lost in forests, and ones desperate to escape marrying the neighboring king's daughter to boot, weren't likely to come along very often. Personally, I saw no reason not to take advantage of the one we had, though I had to admit that the phrase "take advantage of" had a somewhat unfortunate ring, given what I was so eagerly proposing.

"The wizard who put you here turned love into a prison," I said. "That's not right either."

"So now two wrongs really do make a right? Is that what you're saying?" Rue asked crossly.

She was sitting at her loom, her fingers moving the shuttle back and forth in quick, irritated motions. Mr. Jones watched at her feet, his tail switching back and forth, waiting for the opportunity to pounce.

"Of course not," I confessed. "I'm just trying to point out that it's not always possible to see the end of something at its start."

"Very poetic," Rue said. She gave the shuttle another shove. Mr. Jones's head followed the movement of the shuttle. "But poetry is just words."

"You see, that's just what I mean!" I cried. "That's just the sort of thing I said to Alex, to Prince Alexander, last night. All you have to do is talk to him the same way you talk to me, and he'll never know the difference between us.

"Just go out and meet him," I urged. "Please, Rue. We're running out of time. I know this plan isn't beautiful and noble, but it's the only one we've got."

She was silent, frowning at the loom, but I noticed her fingers moved the shuttle more smoothly now.

"You realize this means you'd owe me a favor," she said. "This is twice you've asked for something now. I've only asked you for one thing. You'd be in my debt."

"I don't think that's quite the way it's supposed to work between friends," I said.

"Friends," she echoed, and she turned her head and looked at me with those violet eyes. "Friends," she said again. "Is that what we are?"

"Maybe not yet," I acknowledged. "But isn't that what we're working toward?"

"I honestly don't know," she said. "I guess so." She stopped weaving altogether. The second she stopped moving, Mr. Jones jumped. For a moment I feared he was aiming for the loom. But instead he landed on Rue's lap, turning around three times, then settling in right where he was. I watched as her fingers absently stroked his fur.

"Waking up is hard work," she admitted after a moment. "Harder than I thought it would be. I was picturing—oh, I don't know—something more glamorous and a whole lot easier, I suppose."

"Sort of like a knight in shining armor?" I supplied.

She smiled at that, a smile that matched her name. A rueful smile. "It's just a dream," she said.

"Maybe," I answered. "Maybe not. Maybe all young men who love us become knights in shining armor when we love them back. Even if they don't, Prince Alexander comes pretty close all on his own."

"But he thinks he loves you," she protested.

"Of course he thinks he loves me," I said. "He thinks that I'm a damsel in distress, trapped by enchantment in this tower. I'm not, and we both know it. I'm the one who stayed here of her own free will. You're the one who's trapped. So which one of us does he think he's in love with now?"

"You're giving me a headache, Rapunzel," Rue said.

"It's one of my best talents," I said. "And that was a yes, wasn't it?"

She bent over then and buried her face in Mr. Jones's copper-colored fur. "Yes, that's a yes," she said after a moment. "I will meet this prince of yours."

"Of yours," I said firmly, as I got to my feet. "And remember, he likes to be called Alex."

She didn't speak again, not right away, but as we watched the sun go down in a blaze of orange in the river, I could swear I heard her practicing.

"Alex," she whispered. "Alex. Alex. Alex."

Sixteen

"I thought you weren't coming."

Of course I was coming, I opened my mouth to say. I was standing on the tower balcony, halfway between the windows and the railing, close enough to hear Alexander's voice but still be out of sight.

I've been looking forward to seeing you all day. Besides, it's not as if I have much else to do. I'm trapped up here, if you recall.

But instead, I bit down on the tip of my tongue and said nothing. For now it was Rue's turn to speak, to put in motion a sequence of events that would awaken her heart, win her a prince's love, and gain back her freedom, all at the same time. All she had to do was open her mouth and speak to Alex.

As opposed to what she was doing right this very moment, which was standing in one of the balcony's big casement windows, neither quite inside nor out, behaving precisely as if she'd just come down with a terminal case of laryngitis.

"Don't just stand there," I hissed over my shoulder. "Come out where he can see you. Say something."

"In a minute," she hissed back. "I'm working up to it. Don't rush me."

"I know you're there," Alexander called up. "Look, I brought a torch. Now we'll be able to see each other."

And the soldiers, if they're still around, will be able to spot you, I thought. *I'll bet Harry had a hand in this.*

"Just walk forward, as slowly as you like, until you reach the railing," I whispered to Rue. "Go see what he looks like. Trust me, the moment he sees you, matters will start to take care of themselves."

"You don't know that," Rue whispered back.

Oh, yes I do, I thought. "If you don't come out on your own two feet, I'm going to drag you out by your hair," I said.

"You wouldn't," Rue breathed. "My hair weighs more than you do. You're not strong enough."

"Look," I said, grasping my patience firmly with both hands instead of Rue's hair. "Just pretend you're taking medicine. Do it quickly and get it over with. I'm going to count to three."

"All right. All right," Rue said. "I'm coming. There's no need to—"

"Treat you like a child. I know," I said.

She stepped all the way onto the balcony and began to make her way toward the railing, Mr. Jones trailing along behind. As she passed me, I reached out to clasp her hand, then scooped up Mr. Jones. Five steps. Now eight. Now twelve. Then, at last, she stopped, and I saw her hands come up to grip the railing and hold it tightly. Perhaps it was simply the starlight reflecting off of all that golden hair, but it seemed to me that she glimmered like the last glow of twilight.

For fifteen beats of my heart, the same number of steps it had taken Rue to cross the balcony, she looked down, and the prince looked up.

"You are beautiful," Alexander said. "Even more beautiful than I spent all day imagining, my Rapunzel."

No, no! I thought. For, though highly poetical and romantic, it was altogether the wrong thing to say. It accomplished exactly what the sight of Alex had managed to make Rue forget: She was not Rapunzel. She turned abruptly from the railing and took two staggering steps away.

"Where are you going?" Alexander cried, and I could hear the pain and confusion in his voice. "I've waited all day, just as you asked. Now you won't even speak to me. What have I done?"

Without warning, Mr. Jones dug his claws into my unprotected neck. Stifling a cry, I let him go. He bounded across the balcony toward Rue. At the sight of him, her footsteps faltered. She went to one knee and gathered him up into her arms.

"What is it, Rapunzel?" Alexander asked. "Are you unwell?"

Rue lifted her head then, and her dark eyes looked straight into mine. *You are a cruel and selfish creature, Rapunzel,* I thought. For Rue's eyes shimmered with unshed tears. Her heart was well and truly awake now. I had forced it out into the open before it was ready, then left it, defenseless, to fend for itself. All it had taken to wound it had been the sounding of my name.

So I did the only thing I could. The only thing my eyes and heart could see to do, in that dark night.

"I'm fine," I spoke. "It's just—"

"I know I look a little funny," Alex interrupted, the relief plain in his voice. "I'm sorry. I meant to say something, to warn you, but when I saw you, every single thought seemed to go right out of my head."

"There you go, sounding like a prince again," I scolded. "I thought we agreed we didn't need so many pretty words. What really happened?"

"I'm not sure I want to tell you," Alexander said. "It's too embarrassing. Let's just say I'll never make a good forester and leave it at that."

"Very well," I said. "If you say so."

"You're sure you're all right?" he asked again.

"I'm fine, Alex."

"Then come back out where I can see you."

At this, Rue made a distressed sound and shook her head. "I'm sorry. I can't do that," I said. "At least not for a few moments."

"I don't understand you tonight at all," Alexander said. "You seem so different. Don't you want to see me?"

"Of course I do," I said. "But this isn't some courtly game, Alex. You are free to walk away whenever you want, but I am trapped. It will take more than pretty words to set me free."

"I'm sorry," he said. "I didn't mean to sound false. What would you like me to say?"

"Tell me how you spent your day," I said.

"I made a friend," he replied at once, then laughed. Rue's head tilted toward the sound. "Listen to me," he said. "I sound like a five-year-old."

"A friend. That sounds promising. I'm happy to think you're not alone."

"His name is Harry," Alexander said. "I'm not so sure he thinks very much of me. He spent most of the day mumbling about useless princelings who can't see what's right in front of them. It has to do with what happened to my face. I think he was trying to be insulting."

Rue had turned her head to one side now, as if the better to hear Alexander's voice.

This can still work, I told myself. *Just keep talking.*

"Yet you call him a friend," I commented.

"I do," Alex said, and he laughed once more. "He may not think much of me, but I like him. He's certainly a change from fawning courtiers and mealy-mouthed ambassadors. He has said that I may stay with him in the woodcutter's cottage, but not if I expect to be waited on. I wanted him to come with me tonight, so that I could introduce him. But he claims it's unnecessary, for you've already met."

"I have met Harry," I said.

"How long have you been in this place?" Alex suddenly asked, and I saw Rue wince.

"I'm not sure I know," I answered. "I don't think time has always moved in the same way for me as it has for everyone else."

"Have you no companions?" Alex asked.

"I have a cat named Mr. Jones," I said.

There was a beat of silence.

"I think," Alexander said at last, "that life in your tower must be very lonely. I meant what I said. I would like to find the way to free you."

"Because you feel sorry for me," I said.

"Because I love you," he answered.

I heard Rue pull in one shaking breath.

"How can you love me?" I asked. "We just met. Do you think love is a first impression and nothing more?"

"Of course not," Alexander said. "I have seen love. I can hardly claim to be an expert, but I think I know the real thing when I see it."

"Where have you seen love?" I asked. For it came to me, in that moment, that I had never seen it for myself. Not the kind of love I wished for Rue, anyway. Nor the kind I wished for myself.

"There is a tale in my country," Alex said, by way of answer. "It is told to old people when they fall ill. Young ones hear it as they fall asleep at night. It tells of the days when a blight hung over our land. Nothing prospered. Nothing flourished. Not even zucchini would grow."

"It must have been a terrible blight indeed, if that were true," I said without thinking. Alex laughed, and it was a joyful sound.

"To tell you the truth," he confided, "I've never liked zucchini very much. But it does grow just about anywhere, so you have some sense of how bad things were."

"I do," I said. "I'm sorry for interrupting. Please, go on."

"The king of that time decided there was only one remedy," Alex continued. "He must marry his son to the wealthiest princess he could find, and hope that her dowry would help provide the means to bring the country back to life. This king's son was much more dutiful than I am. He met the girl his father had chosen on one day, married her on the second, and on the third, he brought her home to his castle, which was not much more than a pile of drafty stone. The princess took one look at it and said, 'I am now your wife. I have promised to honor and to cherish you, though I never promised to obey, for I have a mind of my own. Most of all, I have promised that I will find the way to love you truly. This, though I hardly even know you, for our acquaintance is no more than three days old. For these promises that I have made, and the ones you made in return, all on behalf of others, I would like to ask you to grant me one wish for myself alone.'

"'You have but to name it,' the newly wedded prince replied. Which was the gallant thing to say, if not the cautious one.

"'I wish you to build me a room,' his wife said. 'One single room where I will be warm in winter, and cool in summer. A room that will ring with my laughter, but where I will not be afraid to rage and cry. A room so well made I can trust that it will shelter me when all others fail, in which our children may be conceived and born. You must do this with your own two hands, for it is not a task that may be entrusted to any other. Will you grant me this wish?'

"The prince was understandably startled at this request. He had been taught to do many things, but building a room of any sort had hardly been among them. The truth was that he did not know how. But as he stood pondering how to answer, he discovered that he did know one thing: He knew how much he wanted to try. For the wish that had been growing in his heart all the while his wife had spoken was that he might prove worthy of whatever she might ask. And so he said, 'Madam, I am not certain I know how to grant this wish, but I am certain that I will try.'

"'That answer will suffice for now,' his bride said. And so, together, they went into the castle, and on their way in, the prince reached down and picked up a single stone.

"For many years the prince worked on the room his wife had wished for. Years that saw him become king, that saw his own sons and daughters born into the world to be princes and princesses. Years that saw his hair turn gray even as his kindom prospered. For the people of the land, inspired by their monarch's dedication, set about following his example. All they did, they strove to do well.

"There were many days when the king could do

no work on the room at all. On those days, he would wrap his fingers tightly around the stone he had picked up on the day his wife had made her wish, as if, simply by touching this small piece of rock, he could make the room she had wished for grow. And, when, at long last, the day came when the king prepared to leave this life, on that day he turned to his wife with tears in his eyes.

"'I have loved you above all else,' he said. 'But still I have failed you, for the only thing you ever asked of me, a single room, remains undone.'

"'Great, foolish heart,' the queen replied. 'How can one so wise still be so blind? You have worked to build me what I asked for all the days of our lives. Even when the task seemed impossible, even when it would have been easier to give it up, you did not, but kept on going. You have kept me warm in winter, and cool in summer. You have laughed with me, and you have cried. You have given me the children who are almost, but not quite, my greatest joy.

"'For the greatest joy of all is the way you held my wish in the center of your heart through all the days of our lives. That is where the room that you have built for me lies. Just as the room I built for you lies within mine. And in this way have all our wishes been granted. Together, we have made ourselves a home.'

"Not long after this, the king died. Within the space of a year, his queen had followed, and the people mourned. But the tale of the young prince who set out to grant his new bride's single wish is still told to this day, and it inspires all who hear it.

"Do I think that love is no more than a first impression? No, I do not," Alexander said. "But I think that all love must start somewhere, and that place may be no more than the blink of an eye."

Oh, yes, I thought. For I was all but certain that I could see it for myself now. The way to free Rue. The way to free myself. The way to free love.

"Who were they?" I asked. "The king and queen in your story."

"My great-grandparents," Alexander said. "Their portraits hang behind my parents' thrones."

"And you're sure you don't want to marry that neighboring princess?" I asked. "Perhaps your father is only hoping that lightning will strike twice."

"Quite sure, thank you," Alexander replied. "Besides, it's too late. Lightning may indeed strike twice, but I fear it has already struck. I will have no bride but you, Rapunzel. That much my eyes, and my heart, have told me tonight."

There! I thought. Now all I had to do was prove to Rue that I was right.

"Did you hear that?" I whispered to Rue, who had been listening, her face bowed down over Mr. Jones's copper-colored fur, all this while.

"I heard," she murmured. "I heard him call me by your name. He calls me Rapunzel."

"Of course he calls you Rapunzel," I said. "It's the only name he knows. But he loves you."

At this, her head came up. "You don't know that," she whispered fiercely. "You don't *know*."

"Yes, I do," I said. "And I think I know the way to show you."

Grateful that I'd had the presence of mind to wrap myself in a dark cloak, I dropped to my knees and began to crawl forward. Illuminated by the light of the torch below, Alex should be easy to see. But I should blend into the night sky, for I had no golden hair to reflect the starlight.

"Rapunzel," Rue hissed, and she reached out and gripped me by the arm.

"Do you want to know, or don't you?" I asked. "This is it. There's only tonight. Let me do this. If I'm wrong, you can say 'I told you so' for the rest of our lives. I'm not even certain this is going to work, if that makes you feel any better."

"It doesn't," she said, but she let go of my arm. I scooted forward another few inches. I was almost to the railing now.

"You don't answer," Alexander said, and I could hear both pain and wonder in his voice. "Is it that you don't believe me, or that you don't want my love?"

"Answer the question," I hissed over my shoulder, and saw the quick gleam of her hair as Rue whipped her head around.

"*What?*" she cried, then clapped a hand across her mouth. But by then it was too late, for she'd spoken aloud.

"It was hardly a trick question," Alex said. "I've

said I want to marry you, and I mean it truly. You don't answer. Either you don't believe me, or you don't want my love."

"Just do it, Rue," I whispered. "Talk to him. You're going to have to do it sometime. Don't think. Just say what's in your heart."

"What if there's nothing there?" she asked.

"Of course something's there," I answered. "If there wasn't, why on earth would this be so hard? Don't make me count to three again."

"I hate you," she whispered.

"I know you do," I whispered back. Then I turned around and continued to crawl toward the railing.

"You think life is as simple as that?" I suddenly heard her voice lift. "The answers to important questions must be either yes or no?"

Oh, bravo, Rue, I thought. For surely it was better to meet anything—even love, or its loss—head on.

"Of course I don't," Alex protested. "It's just . . . I said I want to marry you. Doesn't that mean anything?"

"It does," Rue replied at once. "But first you have to get me out of here. And second . . ."

"What?"

That was the moment I finally reached my destination. I got to the railing and peered down. At the base of the tower, a torch blazed brightly. Beside it stood a young man, head thrown back, his hands on his hips and his face tilted upward. I could see a great bruise running down one cheek, precisely as if he'd done the thing I knew he had, run it straight into a tree trunk. His eyes sparkled as they caught the torchlight, and his hair shone like a polished copper kettle.

Like Mr. Jones, I thought, and made no attempt to hold back the smile. And then I had no time for any thoughts at all, for he looked up, and I discovered that I could do what I'd hoped: I could see into Prince Alexander's heart.

Almost I looked away, for what I saw was blinding. A light golden and pure, without beginning or end, like looking straight into the sun. I blinked and it seemed to me that I saw a face. It was no more than an ivory oval, outlined by all that gold, but I thought I knew to whom it belonged. Never static, never still. Not the face of a beloved, set in stone, but set in light. A light that held the dreams of the future, the limitless possibilities.

That was what Alexander had seen when he looked into Rue's face. The seed of love, planted in the blink of an eye. Yet from this no-more-than-an-instant beginning could grow a thing that would last the course of a lifetime. Nourished and tended like a plant in a garden. Built like the room for which his great-grandmother had wished, one stone at a time.

That is what love is, I thought. A possibility that becomes a choice. A choice you keep making, over and over. Day after day. Year after year. Time after time. And in that moment, I knew what I was seeing. Not simply Rue's face, though that was where it all began, but the very face of love itself.

And so, my eyes full of what I had found within Alexander's heart, I turned my head and looked into Rue's eyes.

I heard her catch her breath, then release it on one long, slow sigh. As if all her questions were being answered. And so I blinked again, and looked into her heart.

Rue's heart was a great confusion, and all of it caged and desperate to be let out. I heard a sound inside my head like the beat of frantic bird wings. The sound of footsteps going first down a great spiral staircase of stone, then back up again. Down and up. Down and up. Round and round. Round and round. I heard the sound her shuttle made as she pushed it back and forth.

But in the very center of her heart, no sound at all, only a single candle flame of light. A light I thought that I had seen, just once before. The light that had convinced me to stay with her in the first place. Rue's own hope, which—in spite of all the years she had spent relegated to the background of the only heart that knew of her existence—had still found the way to shine.

It was not as bright as the light in Alexander's heart. Not yet, but that didn't make it any less strong. For it had weathered storms his heart could never imagine and not gone out. In the very center of her heart, against all odds and misguided magic, Rue had kept alive the hope of love.

I closed my eyes then, and my visions vanished. I

was just a girl in a dark cloak crouched at the top of an enchanted tower, and the wind blew all around.

"What's the second thing?" I heard Alexander ask. "Just tell me, and I'll try to accomplish it, whatever it is."

I opened my eyes and looked at Rue. She looked back, straight into my eyes. For a moment, the whole world seemed to fall away, leaving just the two of us at the top of the tower.

"There is a question that I have asked myself all my life," I said softly. "Though I have always known that I would never have an answer for it. I've wondered what it might be like to have hair. Shining, golden hair. Hair just like yours, though even I never imagined quite so much of it. You can give me the next best thing, if you will."

"How?" she whispered. "I don't see how."

"Don't leave this place as Rue," I said. "Leave it as Rapunzel. Rue was never your true name, but only the name of your mother's regret, and your own sorrow. Is that how you want to begin a new life?"

"No," Rue said. "No, it's not. But who will you be, if I am Rapunzel?"

"The same person I have always been," I said. "Only now my name can be one that I have chosen. From this day forward, if you are willing, when people speak of the longest, most beautiful golden hair in all the world, the name they speak will be Rapunzel. You would be giving me a very great gift. But only if that is what you wish to choose."

"Let me think," Rue said, and I could have sworn

I saw a smile play at the corners of her mouth. "I can have my freedom and someone to love if I will take your name in the bargain?"

"Something like that," I acknowledged. "So what do you say? Is it a deal?"

"Oh, yes," Rue said. "I think so."

"Then tell your impatient prince the second thing that he must do," I said. "And so accomplish the first one in the bargain."

"All I wish," she said, raising her voice so that Alexander might hear, "is to be asked, rather than told."

"Is that all?" Alexander said.

"That is all," she replied.

"In that case, will you please marry me, Rapunzel?" Prince Alexander asked.

And the girl who would now carry my name for all the ages, the girl with the shining golden hair, answered.

"Yes."

SEVENTEEN

"You could have told me," Harry said several days later as we walked beside the river. "I can keep a secret, you know."

"I see," I said. "That wouldn't be anything like the way you can trust me, would it?" I watched as a dull flush slowly made its way across his cheekbones.

"I've said I was sorry about that. More than once. How many more times would you like me to say it?"

"I don't know," I answered. "I'm still working that out. You hurt me, you know."

"I do know that," he said. "As I've said until I'm almost blue in the face, I'm sorry, Parsley. I never meant . . . Oh, for pity's sake," he suddenly exclaimed. "This is completely ridiculous. I don't even know what to call you."

"I've been working on that," I said, with a smile. "And I think I've come up with something."

"Just so long as it isn't Fenugreek," Harry said.

I laughed and slipped a hand into the crook of his arm.

It had been almost a week now since I had ceased to be Rapunzel. Days full of wonder that had seemed to fly by. No sooner had Rue accepted Alex's proposal than she and I were freed in a great burst of magic that lasted, as you can probably guess, no longer than the blink of an eye. Though it could have taken longer, I suppose. For the truth is that the experience was so overwhelming I kept my own eyes closed through most of it.

The tower first began to tremble, and then to shake, and then, with a sound like a thousand birds in flight, the whole edifice had come tumbling down. I had the sensation of falling head over heels, then landing lightly on my feet, through absolutely no effort I made myself. By the time I could bring myself to open my eyes again, I was standing on the greensward, which was now the size of a small meadow. At my back was the river, and where the tower had stood there was now a snug stone cottage with a slate roof and a bright red door.

Into each side was set a cunning curve of windows, which sparkled like stars. Later I learned that they had retained at least one of their former characteristics. From inside, it seemed that you could see the whole world, if you knew how to look. But from the outside, only your own reflection. The world could come in only if you invited it. Harry was standing in front of the cottage door, blinking rapidly, as if trying to figure out the impossible, which would be how he'd gotten there in the first place. He was holding the cat in his arms.

In the center of the meadow, a great ring of torches set fire to the night. And in the center of that stood Rue—Rapunzel now, of course—and Alex. Beside them was a very startled company of men on horseback. Soldiers, by the looks of them, each and every one with Harry's bemused and slightly alarmed expression on his face, and armed to the teeth besides.

The largest and tallest of them was just getting out of the saddle when I opened my eyes. He took several steps and threw his arms around Alex, lifting him in a hug so fierce he picked him clean up off the ground.

He set him down again and there were several moments of earnest conversation I wasn't quite close enough to hear. I was pretty certain I heard the words "battle" and "neighboring kingdom," and finally the word "magic," at which the king, for surely this could be no other than Alex's own father, gave a great laugh, took two more steps, and lifted Rapunzel off her feet too. And I remembered what Alexander had said, that the neighboring king feared magic of all kinds.

Then Alexander's father turned to his soldiers and, in a voice I was pretty sure was loud enough to be heard back at his own palace, a full day's ride away, said, "I give you Rapunzel, who has saved us from destruction and is to marry my son in three weeks' time."

At this, several more things happened all at once. The soldiers began to cheer. Harry dropped the cat, and I heard a sound like a set of pots and pans doing their best to impersonate a set of wind chimes. Into the meadow came the tinker's cart, with Mr. Jones sitting behind the horse and the sorceress at his side.

While Melisande was busy being reunited with her daughter, not to mention meeting her future son-in-law, the tinker had come to stand at my side.

"You were successful, then," he said.

"So it would seem," I replied.

He put his arm around my shoulders and gave them a squeeze. "I never doubted you would be, you know. I have always believed in the strength of your heart."

"You had more faith in it than I did," I answered.

"No," he said quietly. "I don't think that can be so. For if it were, none of what I see now would be happening. I gather you have given up your name."

I shrugged. "I never really liked it, to tell you the truth."

"What will you be called?"

"I don't quite know. I have something in mind, but I want to think it over a little more first. May I ask you a question?"

"Of course you may," the tinker said.

"Who is the girl that you hold in your heart? I didn't mean to look without permission, honestly I didn't. But I caught a glimpse once, years ago, and I—"

He put both hands on my shoulders, giving me a shake to stop the flow of words.

"Look now," he said. "See if you can answer that question for yourself."

And so, on that night when I thought I had already seen all that love might have to offer, I looked into the tinker's eyes. There was Harry, just as I expected, only now the girl I had seen before was almost at his side. She had but to take one step for them to stand shoulder to shoulder. To reach out to place her hand in his. And I understood that, in the tinker's heart at least, at Harry's side was where the girl belonged. Once more I saw the glint of gold that framed her face, and thought my own heart would crack with grief.

Then she shifted, ever so slightly, and I saw that the gold came from a kerchief with gold-petaled flowers embroidered on it. Flowers with centers as dark as the girl's eyes. And in those eyes, I saw the babe she had once been. I saw the tinker as a young man bow his head over hers as he held her in his arms. I saw him let her go, and what that letting go had cost.

I bowed my own head then, and closed my eyes. The visions wavered and were gone. When I looked back up, the tinker stood before me, only now I saw him truly. Saw what he had been all along.

"If my heart is strong, I inherited it from you," I said. "Father."

"My child," he said.

And then I walked straight into his arms.

The leave-takings began not long after that. For Alexander was understandably eager to introduce his bride-to-be to his mother, and the king wished to get back to the palace before rumors of his strange disappearance grew too dire and his wife too alarmed. Melisande would accompany her daughter to the palace. The tinker, Harry, and I would follow in two weeks' time.

"You are sure?" the girl who carried the name that I had possessed since I first drew breath inquired, as we prepared to part.

"I am sure," I said. "There was never any doubt in my mind."

"You really are impossible," she said.

I reached out and took a strand of that golden hair between my fingers. It was softer and finer than the finest embroidery silk. Not only that, it was the perfect length now. Flowing down her back to swing just above her heels, not quite as long as she was tall.

"Your hair is beautiful, Rapunzel," I said. "I thank you for it with all my heart."

At this, her eyes filled with tears. "I don't know how to thank you," she said. "I don't even know what to call you now."

"I'll tell you at the wedding," I said. "I owe you a cake, as I recall."

"An angel cake as tall as the oven door," she answered with a smile. Then she glanced over my shoulder, to where Harry stood talking with the tinker. "I'd like to say good-bye to Harry, unless you mind."

"Why should I mind?" I asked. At which her smile got a little wider.

"I'm sure I can't imagine," she said.

"Who's being impossible now?"

"Rapunzel tells me you have been a good friend to her," I heard a voice say as she moved away. I turned around and there was Alex.

Oh, you are a fine young prince, I thought. Even with that great bruise darkening one cheek, he was as fine and handsome a prince as any girl trapped in an enchanted tower could want. And he didn't stir my heart. Not one little bit.

"I have done my best," I replied.

He cocked his head then, as if listening to a tune he'd once heard, but whose name he couldn't quite recall.

"Have we met before?"

"You have never seen me before this moment," I answered, choosing my words with care, for I wanted to be honest. "But I will look forward to seeing you again, at your wedding."

He smiled. I watched the way his eyes sought out Rapunzel and stayed there. "She's beautiful, isn't she?" he asked.

"I have never seen anyone more beautiful," I answered, honestly once more.

"You would say this?" he asked, as his eyes flicked back to me. "I thought women were supposed to be jealous of one another."

"That is a tale that men tell to make themselves more important," I said, at which he laughed. "Besides, what's the point of being jealous of love?"

"I see that Rapunzel is right. You are a good friend, for you speak the truth," Alexander answered with a smile.

At that she came to him and took him by the arm. He gave me a bow, the first I had ever received from a prince, and together the two of them moved off.

Finally, the time came to say farewell to the sorceress.

"I don't know what to say to you," she said. "Though there is the obvious, of course."

"The obvious is the obvious because it works just fine," I said.

"I love you," she said simply. "Thank you for freeing my child."

"She did that herself," I said. "I just figured out how."

"She tells me you have inherited my gift," Melisande said. "I'm pleased."

I gave a snort. "It's a little uncomfortable, to tell you the truth. I'm sorry if I was unfair before."

But Melisande shook her head.

"I would like you to know this: I never let you call me Mother because I feared that if you did, when the time came, as I knew it would, I would never have the strength to let you go. But I have loved you no less than the daughter I nurtured with my blood. You have lived inside my heart from the moment my eyes first beheld you. You have been mine from the first time I held you in my arms."

"I know that," I said. "I know it. Mr. Jones tells me

that the woman who bore me died not long after I was born. Her heart simply could not find the way to beat, the doctors said. Perhaps the hole she had made in it was too wide."

"I hope you will call me Mother from this day forward," Melisande said.

"Thank you," I answered. "I will do so with much joy."

"Mother!" another voice called out. Melisande and I shared a smile.

"Your daughter Rapunzel is calling you," I said.

"So it would seem," the sorceress replied. "I'll see you at the wedding. I'll even help you beat the egg whites, if you like."

"I'll hold you to that promise," I said.

Then I watched as they rode away into the dawn.

Eighteen

It began with a theft and ended with a gift. And in between came an illusion, a sleight of hand, a choice that became the chance for love. For that is all we can see in just one blink of an eye. Love's possibility; its outline. After that, it's best to pick up a stone and put it in your pocket, to remind you of what you're trying to accomplish, what you're trying to build: a home inside your heart, a love that lasts a lifetime.

For Alex, it was a girl with shining golden hair, never mind what that girl was called. For me, it was a tinker's boy named Harry. And for Harry—I should tell you how we ended up, shouldn't I?

We lived happily ever after, of course. As did Rapunzel and Alexander—and to the end of his days, she called him Alex.

What did Harry call me?

I'll tell you that as well.

After we had walked beside the river on that long-ago day, after all the others save the two Mr. Joneses had departed, we came to a place where a great rock sat in the center of the slow-moving current. I hitched up my skirts and waded out to it.

"What are you doing?" Harry asked. "Where are you going?"

"I'm going to sit on this rock," I said. "And, if you come too, I will both ask and tell you something. If you stay right where you are, you can just forget about it."

He gave a great sigh and waded out with much stomping and sloshing. But I knew him well enough by this time. I let him have his say with his legs and feet, and said nothing until he'd plopped down beside me. Then I took off my kerchief, the first that he had given me and still my favorite, the one with the black-eyed Susans embroidered on it. I held it in my lap, leaned out over the water to gaze at my reflection, and said, "This is what I look like."

"What are you talking about?" he said, his voice as cross as his legs had been. "Of course that's what you look like. That's what you've always looked like, more or less."

"I am not ever going to grow hair," I said. "In particular, I am not ever going to grow lovely, long, and flowing golden hair such as adorns the head of the girl who will now go through life being called Rapunzel."

"I still don't understand why you let her do that," Harry said.

"I didn't let her do it. I asked her to do it."

"*What?*"

"How would you rather be remembered?" I asked. "As the girl with the golden hair, or the girl who was bald as an egg?"

"Neither, if you want to know."

I gave him a push that would have sent him straight into the water if he hadn't known me well enough to brace himself first.

"You know perfectly well what I mean," I said.

"I don't care about your hair. Your lack of hair." He made an exasperated sound and dragged a hand through his own. "I've never cared about it. Is that what you're trying to ask?"

"Sort of," I said.

He leaned over and took me by the shoulders, turning me to face him. "I am only going to say this once, Parsley, so I hope you're paying attention. When I look at you, I don't see hair or no hair. I just see you."

"You kissed me. Why did you kiss me?" I asked.

"Not even you can be that stupid," he said. "Why do you think?"

And then he did it again.

His lips were impatient and just a little cool as they moved on mine, for the day was chilly, though it was fine. But the hands that held me close were gentle, and, beneath them, I felt my body start to warm. Just like the first time, my heart spoke one word and that was all.

Home, it said. *Home.*

Not very romantic, some of you may be thinking. To which I can only reply that you are the ones who haven't been paying attention. The kiss ended and I rested my face against Harry's chest.

"You make me crazy," he murmured, his lips playing against my smooth head. "You've always made me crazy. Do you know that?"

"I do it on purpose," I said. And felt what it sounded like when he laughed.

"What am I going to do with you?"

"You could marry me," I said. "We could make a home in that stone cottage."

"I could marry who?" Harry asked.

I lifted my head. In my lap I still held the kerchief. I looked down at it and said:

"These are my favorite flowers."

"You told me that when I gave it to you. I know that," Harry said.

"Stop interrupting." I poked him in the stomach with one finger, and he sucked in a breath. "They're called black-eyed Susans."

"So?" Harry asked, but I thought I could see the beginnings of a smile play around the corners of his mouth. He was quick. He'd always been so quick. Quick and stubborn, with hair the color of mud and eyes like the promise of spring.

"Now who's making who crazy on purpose?" I asked.

"Susan," he said. "You want to be called Susan, am I getting this right?"

"I do," I said. "It's a good name. A straightforward name. A no-nonsense name with backbone."

"And it's not some nasty-tasting herb," Harry put in.

"It's not any kind of herb at all," I said. "So what do you think?"

"I think I love you whatever you're called, but I will call you Susan if that's what you wish."

"And you'll never call me Parsley again, right?"

"Oh, no. No promises about that," Harry said.

"Now wait just a minute, Harry," I began.

He reached over and gave me a push. I wasn't quite as quick as he had been. I hadn't braced myself, but I did grab him on the way down. We tumbled into the river together. Fortunately, it was shallow.

"So," I suddenly heard Mr. Jones call. "You've decided to live happily ever after."

"Looks that way, doesn't it?" Harry called back. He grinned down at me, and, in spite of the fact that I was soaking wet with small, sharp stones digging into my back, I felt my heart give a great roll inside my chest.

"Her name is Susan, in case you've been wondering," Harry said.

"Of course it is," Mr. Jones said. "Now come inside. It's time for supper."

"In a minute," Harry said.

He kissed me again, of course, until I could no longer tell whether the sound in my ears was the rushing of the water or my own blood.

"Marry me," he whispered. "Marry me soon."

"Yes," I whispered back. "Yes."

He let me up then. He pulled me to my feet and kept my hand in his as we waded back to shore. Just before we got there, he bent and picked up two stones, holding them out in the flat of his palm.

"You sneak!" I exclaimed. "I knew you were listening."

"Pick one," he said.

So I chose one, and Harry kept the other. And, though no one ever tells the tale of a girl named Susan and a boy named Harry, we have been living happily ever after, building the room that is our love, our home, inside our hearts from that day to this.

We build it, still, for as long as we draw breath.

Author's Note

Why on earth would anyone decide to write a version of "Rapunzel" and take away her best-known feature? I can explain, honestly.

Several members of my family suffer from alopecia areata, an autoimmune skin disease which can result in the loss of hair on the scalp and elsewhere on the body. It can occur in both women and men of all races. While not life-threatening, it is most certainly life-altering!

A couple of years ago, while home on a family visit, I happened to fall into conversation with one of my brothers-in-law. Both he and his daughter are affected by alopecia. I was mulling aloud over the fact that my editor was interested in a retelling of "Rapunzel." At which point my brother-in-law turned to me and said: Could you do a version of "Rapunzel" where she doesn't have any hair? That was pretty much all it took to get me going.

I suppose you could say that, in addition to the official dedication at the front of the book, this story is also for those affected by alopecia areata. As I hope you found my characters discovered for themselves, beauty isn't merely in the eyes of the beholder. It's also in the heart.

About the Author

CAMERON DOKEY is the author of nearly thirty young adult novels. Her other titles in the Once upon a Time series include *Wild Orchid, Belle, Sunlight and Shadow, Before Midnight, Beauty Sleep,* and *The Storyteller's Daughter.* Her other Simon & Schuster endeavors include a book in the Simon Pulse Romantic Comedies line, *How NOT to Spend Your Senior Year.* Cameron lives in Seattle, Washington.

DON'T MISS A MAGICAL TITLE
IN THE ONCE UPON A TIME SERIES!

THE
ROSE BRIDE

A Retelling of "The White Bride and the Black Bride"

BY NANCY HOLDER

Once upon a time, in the Forested Land, a merchant named Laurent Marchand lived with his second wife, Celestine, and their little daughter, Rose. Laurent toiled endlessly to acquire vast wealth, and Fortune smiled on him. His family lived like nobility in a sprawling slate-roofed *château* that towered above fertile orchards and wild woods teeming with game. They dressed in fine silks and satins and dined on dishes of gold bound with silver. Their servants were happy and counted themselves lucky indeed to work for such a prosperous man.

But as with all forested lands, shadows cast their darkness over the manor on the hill. That was to be expected. Most living things begin in the absence of light: The vine is rooted in the earth; the fawn takes form in the womb of the doe. So it is with secret wounds and heartaches. They can father the greatest happiness—if a brave, shining soul will bear them from the darkness and lift them to the light.

So it is also with the deepest of all joys: a love so true and everlasting that it can heal such wounds. For true love is true magic, as those who have found it can attest.

Laurent's dark, secret wound was named Reginer Marchand. Reginer was Laurent's son by his first wife, who had died giving birth to him. Laurent pinned all his hopes on his heir, waiting for the day when his son would be old enough to help him expand his vast domain. He believed that with

Reginer by his side, he would amass a fortune larger than any he could create alone.

But Reginer wanted to be a painter, not a merchant. He spent days, nights, weeks at his easel, reveling in his artistic vision. Thanks to Laurent's efforts, the family would never run out of money, so why sacrifice his dream on the altar of commerce?

Laurent was infuriated by his son's "disloyalty." Painting was a fine pastime, but there was an estate to manage and trading to do. Anger grew on both sides, and one stormy January night, Laurent and Reginer quarreled violently. Reginer packed a bag and stomped out of the grand house. Biting sleet pierced his ermine cloak, and the winter wind wailed like mourners at a funeral.

"Go! Go and be damned!" Laurent yelled, shaking his fist at his son's retreating back. "Though you starve, though your children beg in the streets, never ask a thing of me! Think of me as your father no longer and never dare to put your hand on my door!"

Heartsick and humiliated, Reginer obeyed his father's command to the letter. Years passed, and he did not return.

When Laurent married his second wife, Celestine, and brought her to the estate, she was sorry to learn of the rift between her new husband and his firstborn. Despite her gentle entreaties, Laurent still refused to forgive Reginer. And as Celestine loved her husband and owed him everything, she promised that she would follow his edict and bar the door to her stepson. But Reginer never came. So the shadow of the wound became invisible, although it was still very real.

The other shadow that fell across the lives of the Marchands was easier to see, although it too, had to do with the aching of the human heart. It was Laurent's near-continuous absence from the beautiful *château* and his family.

"I chase gold as others chase the hare," he boasted to his delicate, fair-haired wife, "and I do so for you and our daughter. My love is such that you will never go wanting."

He didn't understand that Celestine and Rose were sorely wanting indeed: When he was gone, which was more often than not, they missed him terribly. His time and attention were more valuable to them by far than their jewels and dresses. Of a moonlit evening, Celestine would walk along the stony terraces of the *château*, gazing past the topiary garden, the hedge maze, and the chestnut groves to the narrow, winding mountain passes, searching for her husband's retinue. She understood that Laurent loved them, but there were times she felt more widow than wife.

Aside from her beloved child, Celestine's boon companion was Elise Lune, who had served as Celestine's nurse at the family seat on the Emerald Plains. When Celestine married Laurent, the young bride begged Elise to come with her to the Forested Land.

"I shall know no one there," Celestine reminded her. "And one hopes that one will have children, and such tiny blossoms will need tending. . . ."

Elise had no other family and loved Celestine like her own child. So she left the comfort of the Emerald Plains to journey with her young mistress to the Forested Land. She was the first to know that Celestine would have a child and she helped in the delivery of Rose. Many a night she walked the floors of the Marchand mansion, singing lullabies and bouncing the teething child. She was with Celestine when Rose took her first step. And it was she who slipped Celestine's gold coins bearing the likeness of King Henri beneath Rose's pillow whenever the dear girl lost a tooth. She was so beloved that she became *Tante* Elise—Aunt Elise—and the fact that she was a servant slipped from everyone's minds.

When little Rose turned seven, Celestine decided to create a rose garden for her daughter's pleasure. Once the dozens of bushes were planted, Celestine tended them with nearly as much love and devotion as she showered on *la belle* Rose. The roses responded and the garden became an astonishing bower of unearthly beauty, a lush, velvet canopy of crimson hanging over a blanket of scarlet, opulent with heady perfume . . . and they whispered to the distraught girl:

"You are loved.

"You are loved.

"You are loved."